Conflagration

Canadian Historical Mysteries
donalee Moulton

Print ISBNs
Amazon Print 9780228628491
Ingram Spark 9780228628507
BWL Print 9780228628514

BWL Publishing Inc.

Books we love to write …
Authors around the world.

http://bwlpublishing.ca

Series copyright 2023 BWL Publishing Inc.
Novel copyright 2023 donalee Moulton
Cover art by Michelle Lee

Disclaimer

This book is based on a true story, but it is a work of fiction. There are characters, actions, conversations and more that are totally imaginary. The novel centres around the life, arrest, and trial of Marie-Joseph Angélique, an enslaved Black woman accused of committing arson in Montréal in 1734. There may be language used and events depicted that are upsetting and triggering. Please take care when reading.

Canadian Historical Mysteries

Rum Bullets and Cod Fish - Nova Scotia

Sleuthing the Klondike – Yukon

Who Buried Sarah- New Brunswick

The Flying Dutchman – British Columbia

Bad Omen - Nunavut

Spectral Evidence – Newfoundland

The Seance Murders – Saskatchewan

The Canoe Brigade – Quebec

Discarded – Manitoba

Twice Hung - Prince Edward Island

Jessie James' Gold – Ontario

Dedication

For Allan.
For everything.

Acknowledgements

This book exists because of the support of many people.

I want to thank Cheryl Enman for reading and rereading these pages, for honest and frank feedback, and for her unparalleled commitment to the correct use of commas. A heartfelt thank you to Lynn Bruce for discussing the content with me, talking about possible avenues my characters could take, and pushing me to consider paths for them I would otherwise not have contemplated. Hyacinthe Miller, outstanding author and President of the Crime Writers of Canada, read my work with sensitivity and insight and offered invaluable feedback. Before she even turned the first page, Hyacinthe made suggestions that improved the work. I owe a debt of gratitude to my publisher Jude Pittman who offered me this opportunity and introduced me to Marie-Joseph Angélique.

As always, I want to thank my partner, Allan Kindervater, whose support is often unspoken but never wavers. Good day or bad day, he's there, and I am grateful.

I had not heard of Marie-Joseph Angélique until I began this book. That is an individual failing and a societal one. While many, like me, have been unfamiliar with the story of the enslaved Black woman executed for arson in Montreal in 1734, many others have strived to bring her life and death to light through plays, books, videos, and more. I am immensely grateful for their work, their insight, and their commitment to telling Canadians and the world about Angélique and dispelling the myths about slavery in this country. In particular, I want to acknowledge the groundbreaking work of Dr. Afua Cooper in her book *The Hanging of Angélique: The Untold Story of Canadian Slavery and the Burning of Old Montréal*. Dr. Cooper shines an unflinching light on the life and times of Angélique and brings that life and those times into historical perspective. I would also like to recognize the important contribution of the website Great Unsolved Mysteries of Canadian History in helping us understand the realities that shaped Angélique's life and the judicial process that ultimately ended it. Their site, *Torture and Truth: Angélique and the Burning of Montreal,* offers access to court documents in the original French and English translations. This is a vital resource.

In the end, of course, this is a story about Marie-Joseph Angélique. My hope is that this fictionalized account honours Angelique's memory by bringing her story to a new group of readers.

donaleeMoulton

* * *

BWL Publishing Inc. acknowledges the Government of Canada and the Canada Book Fund for their financial support in creating the Canadian Historical Mysteries.

BWL Publishing acknowledges the Province of Alberta for their ongoing support through the Alberta Publisher's Cultural Industry Operating Grant.

Table of Contents

Chapter 1
Montréal
Friday, April 9, 1734

Mud is everywhere. It defines Montréal in April. The snow continues its laborious melt, the ice in the St. Lawrence jostles the shoreline, the clouds hover relentlessly close to earth, and everywhere there is heavy, wet, sticky muck. It adheres to the sides of shoes, the bottoms of coats, and the brims of hats whipped to the ground by winds, there one minute, gone the next.

I look down. My boots are caked in grime, a primordial ooze from the earth, from under the sea, from crevices unknown. I will spend much of this evening cleaning heels, toe caps, and outsoles only to have more mud adhere tomorrow. These caked brown scars are visible reminders that I am not at home. Not at home in this town. Here I have no roots, no history.

Home is Acadie, another world away in another part of New France. My home, admittedly, has mud, but it is the mud pigs roll in to cool their skin, the mud farmers use to build dykes, the mud kids make patties with under the spring sun. Montréal mud is

13

a nuisance, a bother, a reminder of life's inconveniences.

I am feeling sorry for myself. I am missing my family. It happens. I accept the ache, acknowledge its origins, and move forward, literally through more mud. I remind myself of Madeleine, my wife. She makes life in here bearable. She makes life breathable.

The afternoon sun hides behind clouds. But even in disguise, its demise for the day is evident. Soon it will be dark. I need to push onward, deliver these papers, and make my way home before nightfall. Before the mud becomes invisible, and treacherous. The ground is still hard and much of it frozen; mud will not break a fall, but it will cause one. I need to be careful. For Madeleine.

* * *

François de Béréy's home is large by Montréal standards. Indeed, it is large by any standard. It rises three floors in the heart of the merchants' quarter on rue Saint-Paul where it announces its presence to fur traders and aspiring businessmen without saying a word. It sits across from the Hôtel-Dieu de Montréal, the town's convent and hospital. Three sisters in full habit are outside getting, I assume, a much-needed break from the rigors of tending to the ill and the injured. Immediately, I feel guilty for my selfishness, for a little mud. I nod at the three

14

nuns acknowledging their presence and, I hope, their worth. The three women nod back.

I turn away and knock on the door in front of me. A young servant girl answers. She is about seventeen, dark brown hair pulled back in a bun, pleasantly overplump. She wears a white apron. Her head is bowed. "Philippe Archambeau pour Monsieur de Béréy, s'il vous plait."

The young woman scurries off. She is back in a few seconds. She ushers me into the foyer. She does not look at me.

My business is over as quickly as it began. Documents delivered, and my day is done. The sun is struggling with the horizon, and losing. I would like to be home before it cedes the daily battle. I hurry down to the street. Two women are talking at the bottom of the steps, a servant and a Panis slave. They turn their backs to me and continue their conversation. As I walk past, I hear only one word: conflagration.

The Panis woman, likely, I thought, from a tribe south of Montréal, turns in my direction as I pass. It is a vacant look; I doubt she even sees me. But I see her. In two days, I will put a name to her face: Marie-Manon.

* * *

A heavenly aroma greets me as a walk through the front door. We live several streets away from the merchants' quarter, on rue Saint-Antoine, closer to where I work as a court clerk. Madeleine knows somehow today was a long day and a hot beverage will be welcome. The tea, a Bohea blend infused with orange peel, is a special treat. It helps to warm my chilled bones and reassure my feet they will work tomorrow. Madeleine places my boots at the front door. I will tackle them later.

Supper is hot and satisfying, smoked ham with potatoes, cabbage, and onion. More tea follows the meal. As does conversation. This is our time. Madeleine listens with her ears and her heart. This is my favorite time of day.

And I talk about mud. My wife knows I am not really talking about mud but about Montréal, this town that is my home and not my home. "There is mud in Acadie," she says gently. She pats her stomach, almost absently, and reminds me that soon this town will also be the home of our first child.

"I'm sorry." It's the least I can say. What I can do is make our conversation what it should be and what it usually is: meaningful.

"I was in the lower town today."

Madeleine smiles. "I bet it was muddy."

"I saw a Panis slave. My guess, she is from the Fox Nation. Sold to someone here."

"You see slaves every day. Yet you remember this one."

"You are, as usual, right. I saw several slaves today on rue Saint-Paul alone. And a young servant girl. It all disconcerts me still."

I am familiar with slaves. We have slaves in Acadie, but they work the farms, the field, the land as we all do. They seem part of the landscape. Perhaps they do not feel that way. I say this out loud to Madeleine. She does not dismiss the notion as odd as it may be in this town of 3,000 people that includes hundreds of slaves, maybe more.

"Do these slaves look differently to you? Do they act differently?"

They do not, and they do. "It is the vacant stares, the abbreviated eye contact. It does not sit well in my heart."

"Another cup of tea will solve that."

I will come to realize that what I see is the look of those imprisoned. It is the face of those who have no means of escape. Later I will associate it with the wall that surrounds Montréal. I hate that wall. It closes me in. It is supposed to make me feel safe. It doesn't.

* * *

Madeleine is sleeping. She sleeps a lot these days. I understand her body needs this even though she fights it. My mother also slept when she was with child, my brothers and sisters.

I take the last of the tea, reheated on the hearth. Madeleine would not approve. She would make a fresh pot, and we would talk. Tonight, she sleeps, and I look at the stars.

They are the same stars I see in Acadie. And they are not.

From my front door, from most front doors, the wall is not visible. It is as if it does not exist. But we all know it surrounds us. Or almost surrounds us. For nearly twenty years, Gaspard-Joseph Chaussegros de Léry has planned, managed, and propelled the building of ramparts literally designed to protect Montréal from its enemies, primarily the British. New France's chief engineer will see this wall finished, this town cocooned in stone.

The wall is flanked. Anyone who dares attack Montréal will know what faces them before they ever arrive at these ramparts. That is deliberate, and doable in large part because the town lies on moderately flat land. Curtain walls and strongholds and drawbridges and posterns span 3,500 metres. We are fortified in black limestone and grey crystalline.

The wall speaks to the power of France, and to the consideration of our King, Louis XV, and his famous great grandfather before him. It exudes authority.

It also promotes the trades. Montréal is flourishing inside these ramparts. The wall requires stone fitters and masons. Sawyers and blacksmiths and haulers are also needed. There is enterprise in the rise of these enclosures.

The wall speaks as well to those who seek to make money. It says, "You are safe here. Your business will thrive."

With the wall comes commerce, particularly fur trading. Businesses spring up around this endeavour. Indeed, Montréal is a trading post. Where there is trade, there is community and the shops, markets, and supports needed to bolster and enshrine a town. In the time since the wooden palisade that once circled Montréal was replaced with this new wall, approximately 400 houses have been constructed. And the wall is not yet finished.

Of course, prosperity requires judicial overwatch. Our courthouse bustles with the legal business of business. It also punishes, as it must, those who dare to defy the King's laws. I know this firsthand. I sit each day in that courthouse. I record the testimony of those who walk through its doors. Many faces are familiar. Many are unknown.

None will leave as great an impression as the twenty-five who will walk through its doors in the next twenty-two days.

Chapter 2
Conflagration
Saturday, April 10, 1734

The mud is still everywhere, but the sun is battling with clouds – and winning. It is a lovely spring day; there is warmth, and the town glows. People smile as they walk past each other. They wave. *Bonjour*. Summer is around the corner, and our spirits are soaring.

On days like today, I am reminded of the youthfulness and vibrancy of Montréal. It was less than a hundred years ago that Paul de Chomedey de Maisonneuve and Jeanne Mance founded Ville-Marie as a missionary colony. The fur trade, however, soon became a way of life, and the lifeblood of this town. It is a town that, sadly, is built on blood. The Iroquois and the French battled for decades before the 1,200 troops sent by King Louis XIV put an end to the conflict. La Grande Paix treaty brought peace to our people and the 30 tribes that call this land their home.

I am reminded of how far we have come from the fighting that once dominated this place. I think of the Panis slave I saw yesterday in the lower town. I think of her stare, and I think that perhaps we have not come as far as it would appear on the surface.

* * *

There is much work to be done. As always. The courthouse is a busy place. It sits in the upper town, a visible reminder that the arm of France reaches across the ocean and resides here. Nearby are the parish church and the seminary, the town hall, and, of course, the prison. I have been to the prison to record the testimony of those behind its bars. It is not a pleasant place. There are only two cells, and they are cramped. Movement is not encouraged, and some would say virtually impossible. They are dark and dirty, filled with rats, insects, and other animals that thrive in the underbelly. I do not talk of this with Madeleine.

Today, I am in court. It is a simple trial, as most are. The facts are clear. A man, an engagé, under contract for three years to a merchant in the lower town is accused of stealing two livres from his employer. The two silver coins were found on him. His employer, I write carefully in my notes, saw the man enter his office. The money was missing when the merchant next checked.

The accused will be given an opportunity to respond to the accusation. Judge Pierre Raimbault, the town's highest judicial authority, is always thorough. With the King's prosecutor, he will speak with all the witnesses. He will speak with the accused. He will weigh what he hears and render a verdict. I know the outcome before the trial begins. There is no doubt; the engagé is guilty.

There is part of me that feels badly for this man I do not know. I suspect he served in the military as most of the men under contract did. Why this man chose not to return to France I do not yet know; I may never know. Such information is not essential for my notes, and if the question is not asked, there will be no employment record for this person. This thief.

* * *

We are home from evening mass, something we have been attending more regularly now that Madeleine is with child. It is important to introduce our offspring to God. The evening is pleasant, and our spirits are high. Today was a good day. The trial is going well, and recording was straightforward. It often isn't. Many factors can interfere, including language. I fear the British have influenced my French. This is what comes from living so closely to one another for so long. It may also be the isolation of Acadie from France. We develop our own language. In court, there are different accents, and some people mumble. Oooh, the mumblers.

Madeleine has decided that tonight we will celebrate. We're having our own variation of posset, a drink we first learned of through the British. We heat the milk, add sugar, wine, and spices. The aroma is magnificent. I find myself smiling. Life is good. I must remind myself of this more often. Perhaps, like the British influence that crept into my life when I wasn't looking, Montréal is becoming home without me realizing it.

I start to tell Madeleine about the trial. I don't know if she is really interested in the process and the legalities or if she just wants to hear the sound of a voice as she relaxes and sips her posset.

Her relaxation and my tale are short lived. The parish bells start to toll. I stand up quickly and rush to the door. In the distance, the sky is awash in a blaze of reds, oranges, and yellows. Madeleine is at my side. She holds her stomach protectively. I take her in my arms. Something is wrong. Very wrong.

* * *

The soldiers are beating a warning on drums that can be heard throughout the streets. Soon troops are running through town with buckets, ladders, shovels. The town crier can be heard in the distance. He says only one word, over and over and over.
Fire.

My boots are on, and I am heading out the door. It is the law. All able-bodied men must report to the scene of the conflagration to assist. I take a cloth to wrap around my mouth. The smoke is starting to fill the streets, and it will be intense the closer I get to the blaze.

I turn to kiss Madeleine goodbye. She has a shawl on. "Where are you going?"

"With you."

"Absolutely not. You can't fight a fire."

"But I can help those in distress." With that my wife and my unborn child are out the door and heading down rue Saint-Antoine. I look at her retreating back, proud and perturbed.

We follow the crowd, the drums, and the voice of the town crier to rue Saint-Paul. The street is in flames. The de Béréy house is consumed. It was only yesterday I stood inside that home, admired its design and its furniture, spoke with its owner.

We form a brigade; bucket after bucket after bucket of water is passed and poured on houses that line both sides of the street. To no avail.

In less than three hours it is over. The fire has won. More than forty homes are gone. Gone. Reduced to black ash, burnt stubs of wood, and tar, from the water that was tossed everywhere in a futile attempt to squelch the flames.

Also burnt to the ground – again – is the Hôtel-Dieu de Montréal. The sisters who run this convent and hospital are outside helping those who have sought refuge. A few buildings remain to offer sanctuary including a private courtyard, a small chapel, and a garden. People gather here, at what is often considered to be the heartbeat of Montréal. Mercifully, no one is seriously hurt. No one has died. But families are without homes, their servants and slaves displaced. Businesses destroyed. I see the Panis slave from the de Béréy house and the servant girl who answered the door. They are drinking tea; others are drinking sweetened brandy. They all look past me.

Neighbors and nuns are handing out blankets and offering comfort. Fortunately, the night is mild, wrapped now in a layer of damp smoke. I look from across the street at the human remnants of the fire, at the sisters who scurry to lend aid, at the neighbor woman who holds a child while its mother consoles another. I lock eyes with the neighbor woman through the heavy haze. I know those eyes.

Madeleine.

* * *

We start to make our way home slowly. Our bodies are heavy; our hearts carry the same load. I have never experienced a fire like this. We have been warned, of course, but those warnings pale in comparison to the reality. There is solace only in knowing that we did all we could as a community. I wonder, somewhere in the recesses of my mind, if we did all we legally could have done. But that is a question for another time. Now is the time to mourn what has been lost.

I hold Madeleine's hand. We are about to leave rue Saint-Paul behind us when we hear banging of the drums. François Roy, the town crier, has an announcement. It is perhaps more devastating than the debris and ash that surrounds us.

Marie-Joseph Angélique, Black slave of Thérèse de Couagne de Francheville, set the town of Montréal on fire.

Before there is time to think, to absorb this news, a man in the hospital courtyard turns to the slave woman at the centre of the firestorm. He, too, accuses her of setting the fire, insists everyone knows this. I see people nod their heads. I anticipate their will be trouble.

There isn't. Marie-Jospeh Angélique confronts her accuser. There is no vacant stare, no deference here. No one, she says, would be so stupid as to light their own home on fire.

There is merit in the argument. I wonder if it is an argument that would win out in a court of law. I will soon find out.

Chapter 3
Accused
Sunday. April 11, 1734

There will be no rest tonight, for me, for Madeleine, for our child, for our town. We hear voices throughout most of the early morning hours. People are awake with the sun; some have not yet been to sleep. There will be much to do today for everyone. Superiors in Québec City must be informed. That is a first order of business. I imagine there has been no slumber for Montréal Governor Josué Dubois Berthelot de Beaucours. News of the fire may already be on its way to the capital.

I break fast with some bread and coffee and quietly make my way to the courthouse. I am uncertain whether my trial will continue. *How can it not? How can it possibly?* There is a purposeful air that clings to those in the building. They make their way to rooms with determined stride. I admire the fortitude. I am uncertain how I can help.

My superior, Rolant Huissier, is walking quickly down the hallway. He waves me over. We walk to the main entrance and head outside. Rolant closes the door behind him and looks around.

"Things are not well." I nod, not sure what else is expected of me. "You were on rue Saint-Paul last night. You heard?" I nod again, willing my head to stand still but it bobs of its own accord.

"I tell you in confidence. The procurator has asked for permission to begin an investigation. Permission has been granted. Marie-Joseph Angélique will be arrested today."

I am surprised at the speed of such an arrest, and I am not surprised. "How can I be of assistance?"

"We must ensure we are diligent. All eyes will be on us, on the court, the people of the court. We must be beyond reproach."

I refuse to nod and stop my head before it can complete an entire bob. I wait. Rolant is testing the waters, making sure I am the right person to do what it is he needs someone to do. I want to be that person.

Now Rolant nods. I have passed the test. "You will serve as special rapporteur. It will be your job to look beyond the testimony and the accusations to the evidence. You will serve as a second set of eyes and ears for the court so that when a decision is rendered, it will be with the knowledge that all that could be done was done."

This is an honour. I am humbled. I express my thanks. Rolant looks at me closely. "You have been selected for this task because you are thorough. Your work is beyond question. We will need that dedication more than ever."

I assure my superior I am the man for the job. I believe I am. I know I will do my best. "What would you like me to do?"

"Let us begin with documenting the laws that pertain to fire and adherence with those laws."

This does not seem like the job of a special rapporteur. There is something here my superior is telling me without telling me. I will need to learn to read between the lines.

* * *

Marie-Joseph Angélique is arrested within the hour. There is little fanfare in the streets, yet I hear applause in my mind. This is anticipatory. This is not how a special rapporteur thinks. I reprimand myself, straighten my shoulders and return inside to the courthouse. I gather legal texts, paper, and pen. The courtroom attached to the prison is empty today in the aftermath of the fire, and I stake out a small corner of the room to begin my work.

It doesn't take me long to realize much of my work will lie beyond this room.

* * *

You do not have to be born and raised or even to have lived in Montréal for very long to realize the deadly and destructive threat that fire poses. We saw that last night when much of the merchants' quarter burned to the ground in mere hours. This was not the first time fire ravaged the town, and it was not the worst. On June 19,1721, a fire started at the Hôtel-Dieu and ended with more than 160 houses up in flames.

I read in the archives a recounting of this tragedy by Sister Marie Morin. A gunshot fired in celebration during the feast of Corpus Christi started the blaze.

In an instant, to the roof of the said church and to the vault, which flared up at such great speed that many of our friends present at the time could not extinguish it, although they are quite able and knowledgeable. This caused the alarm to sound to alert people to come to our aid, as it was a lost cause.

A good number appeared at first, but not for long, because the fire also spread to the house where

Sister Morin's words take me back to last night, to the smoke, the heat, the crunch and sizzle of flames as they consumed everything in sight. I also remember the kindness of the sisters and the townsfolk, knowing there were helping hands and kind hearts 13 years ago as there were 13 hours ago. I am bolstered by that thought. I am also aware of what distinguishes our fire from 1721: arson.

The archives are an important place to start. This is not wasting time while I wait for further instructions from Rolant. The fire of 1721 had important consequences for the people who live today in Montréal. Gaspard-Joseph Chaussegros de Léry, chief engineer of New France and overseer of the stone fortifications that ring Montréal, was called on to investigate the blaze. That investigation and de Léry's recommendations led to new laws being put in place to protect the town should fire strike again. As it has.

The law states:

I make a note to look at the shingles, what is left of them, in the lower town. I make another note to check the registry of offences to see if anyone was fined for not cleaning their chimney. Finally, I make a note to purchase a ladder.

* * *

I am not prepared for the destruction. In the dark and the heat and the shock of April 10, I did not see what was right before me. Today, in the light, and the chill, and the weariness of April 11th, destruction is laid bare. The military surrounds much of the ruins, keeping people back for their own safety and for the financial reckoning that will inevitably follow. Some of the families and merchants who lost their homes and stores are allowed past the human blockade to sift through the ashes of their lives. As a court reporter, I am also granted entry.

* * *

I step over remnants of tables and chairs; half a bed juts out from underneath a small mountain of charred wood. Fragments of plates and cups crunch beneath my feet. The head of a hobby horse stares up at me. I look up. Monsieur de Béréy kneels in front of what was once his home. He is making an inventory, salvaging what he can. I look away before he can meet my eyes. *What is there to say?*

I turn to what was once, and still remains, the garden of the Hôtel-Dieu where the nuns would come for solitude and fresh air. Last night this was where the poor, the indentured, the wealthy, the free gathered for a cup of tea, a crust of bread, a comforting hand on their shoulder. Today, there is also a crowd here. I suspect this will be a gathering spot, even lodging, for many of the displaced and homeless for some time to come. A sister strolls by. She nods. I nod back. *What is there is say?*

Women in the community have come to help the sisters, to feed and solace what, but for the grace of God, could have been themselves. A woman bends to give a child a bowl of nourishment. She stops and looks at me. I know those eyes.

My wife walks toward me. She takes a small flask from her pocket, "Drink. You will need this." I do as I'm told. The brandy sears my throat. Madeleine is right. I needed this. I needed to feel.

I smile my thanks. "I didn't even know we owned a flask."

"We don't. This belongs to the sisters. For medicinal purposes."

The laughter bubbles up in my throat, perhaps mixed with the brandy. I don't know. What I do know is that the laughter feels good, feels like hope. A man, mid-rubble, glares at me. I lower my head, chastised. This is not the time or place for laughter. Madeleine squeezes my hand.

"How long have you been here?"

"Since you left this morning. The soldiers opened the storehouse earlier today. We have been distributing supplies." I glance around the garden and see for the first time blankets, barrels, clothes, dishes. Life goes on.

"What will happen?" Madeleine shrugs. There is no answer to that question. I know that as I ask it. Yet the words come out of my mouth of their own will. A need to say aloud what the heart feels inside.

"You are here...?"

"I have news. We will discuss this over supper and coffee this evening. When we can breathe." My wife smiles, perhaps at my newfound decorum or at the prospect of normalcy for a few hours.

"The slave has been arrested."

"I know. In part, that's why I'm here."

"People are saying she threatened to burn Madame de Francheville's home, warned her owner of this, and boasted to others that she would burn the house down."

So, my wife has news. We will discuss this over supper and coffee this evening. When we can breathe.

* * *

I am a court reporter. My job is to record the testimony of witnesses and set down statements from the accused. I am not a soldier; I am not a builder. I do not understand fire. I do not advise those who govern. *What the hell am I doing here?*

I sift through the wreckage that is all that now remains of the lower quarter. I do not know what I am looking for. I am sure it is not the charred paper that clings to my boots or the scorched furs that poke up from beneath blackened remnants of what used to be homes and the commerce carried out in those homes. It is commonplace for merchants to keep their supplies, to conduct their meetings, to trade, to negotiate, to hire and to fire where they also eat and sleep.

That insight, an important reminder of how another class lives, does not help me determine what I am looking for, what I am doing here. I find myself in front of Madame de Francheville's home. If the slave woman started the fire, this is where the first flames sparked. I realize to my surprise the house is next door to Monsieur de Béréy's. If the shingles were the culprit, there would have been little hope of saving the de Béréy home even if the fire could be contained. Wooden shingles are highly flammable and tumble easily in the wind from one roof to another.

Of course, wooden shingles are not legal. The government has seen to that. Regulations prohibit their use, yet still, most of the homes in Montréal have wooden shingles. A few, mostly those belonging to government or the church, have taken steps to protect against fire as demanded of them. Tin roofs. Stone tiles. Slate. Most homeowners, however, have opted for wooden shingles, which are much more affordable and accessible, if illegal. I wonder if there is a fine levied for the use of wooden shingles, then I wonder at the absurdity of that thought. *What does it matter now?*

I am sifting through the remnants scattered on the street although I am not sure why. There is debris and ash and bits and pieces of people's lives everywhere. I bend down to retrieve what remains of a wooden shingle. It looks like it has fallen straight from the de Béréy roof. I am amazed and appalled at the randomness of fire, how some shingles survive a blaze and others wither into char.

This shingle is one of the few on the street. I pick up another. And another. This is all I see. I have no idea why I am collecting shingles, but it feels good to be doing something. The illusion of purpose.

I continue to sift through the detritus. A framed painting has somehow survived, and a silver hair ornament, a brass candlestick. I am running out of carrying space in my arms and coat. I put the shingles aside and take the other finds to the garden. More people have arrived. Madeleine is about to head home. She takes the finds from me and puts them in an area of the garden designated just for this. Families will come here to see what remnants of their home may have been uncovered.

My plan is to walk part way with Madeleine, but I am stopped by the look on a young girl's face. I recognize both the girl and the look. It is Monsieur de Béréy's servant. The dark-haired girl who greeted me two days earlier. It seems like a lifetime ago.

"Are you all right?" She seems somehow thinner, the roundness gone.

The young woman looks at me. This time she seems to see me. She collects herself and lowers her head. "My apologies, monsieur."

"There is nothing to apologize for," I assure her. "Have you eaten?"

She shakes her head "no." Madeleine without a word makes her way to the makeshift kitchen. "My wife will bring you some soup, bread. Sit."

I lead the young woman to one of the many chairs that have somehow materialized in the garden. She sits without a word. A tear makes its way down her cheek. She looks over to the de Béréy house. The house that no longer exists.

As if in answer to my unasked question, she says, "We are going to stay with some relatives of Monsieur de Béréy."

"That is good. You will be warm. You will have food."

The young woman looks through me, perhaps to my wife who has come up behind me. She hands a bowl of soup and some bread to the girl. She also has a blanket. "Madeleine."

The young woman looks into her eyes. "Sidonie."

* * *

Madeleine and I start to walk together toward the upper town. *Shingles.* I remember my find. "One minute," I say to Madeleine and scurry back to the rubble where I have left the burnt wood. Madeleine is amused at my folly. From her perspective,

38

I see the silliness of my finds. I am about to toss the shingles to the ground.

"It gives you purpose," my wife says her hand on my arm.

I love this woman.

* * *

Rolant is waiting for me when I return. He does not ask where I have been or why I am bringing charred wood to the courthouse. I am honoured by his faith in me.

"There have been developments. We need to talk."

* * *

I find an old cloth and lay the three shingles on it in the order I found them. I make a note as to where each shingle was found and the condition of the wood.

Shingle #1. Found in the remains of the de Béréy house under what would have been the stairs leading to the attic. Almost intact. Blackened heavily on one end. Another slash of black a third of the way along. A similar slash near the end of the wood.

Shingle #2. Found about three feet from the first shingle. Charred heavily. Resembles reptilian skin. One corner missing. Top left. Similar black pattern to Shingle #1.

Shingle #3. The blackest of the three shingles. Must be handled with care. It will disintegrate easily. Centre section somewhat stronger. Found in the centre of the street. Unclear whether it has been walked on.

I take my notes and place them carefully aside. I will return here, to these files, frequently over the next few weeks. For now, the filing, indeed the writing of the report itself, is nothing more than busy work. I am preoccupied with what I have learned from Rolant and what this might mean for the case moving forward.

Marie-Jospeh Angélique had a lover. A white lover.

Much of Claude Thibault's life is an open book. Defying the law will do that. There is always documentation. I quickly learn Thibault was born in Butenne in eastern France. He was found guilty of illegally selling salt and given two options: a lifetime in the king's galleys or exile in New France. He chose the latter.

* * *

Thibault spent some time in the military, how much time is not immediately clear from the papers spread before me, but after leaving service he became an indentured servant to François Poulin de Francheville. As an engagé, he worked in the fur trade.

It appears he did not like the work. Or perhaps he loved Angélique. Whatever his motivation, he and the Black slave ran away on February 22 of this year. They did not get far. By March 5, Thibault was in gaol and Angélique was back in the de Francheville house.

This information tells me about the man's life but not much about the man. I will need personal insight for that, not court seals.

* * *

Henri Geôlier is exactly what I would expect a jailer to look like. He is large, burly, bearded. His demeanor is gruff. There is no deference here. I wonder why I expected any. *Because I can write?*

I come with Rolant's name on my lips and bread and cheese in my pocket. We take a moment to eat. Monsieur Geôlier is intent on the food, although he clearly is not going without. I have the decency to blush at this thought. I would have liked to have met in the cells, to have seen the woman accused of burning Montréal, but the jailer, one of two who oversee the prison, is in his private quarters.

He wipes his mouth with the back of his hand. "Thibault is an emmerde." Now, this was not in the court records.

"What made him a pain in the ass?" I want to know.

Monsieur Geôlier rolls his eyes. "Everything."

It turns out Thibault had a mouth on him, and he used it to defy, berate, confront anyone he didn't like or who stood in his way.

"In his way of what?" I'm curious.

"Thibault is French. Not like you and I are French. He detests New France. This place. These people. That hatred boils over."

"Is that why he ran away?"

"He had big plans. Going to the English colonies. Then to France. With what I ask you, little money and a Black woman by his side."

"That would not be easy."

"You don't say. Perhaps that's why he got caught."

The sarcasm is not lost on me. It's not intended to be. I have been put in my place, but my place as special rapporteur is to continue down this path no matter how uncomfortable.

"Do you think he will try to escape again?"

Now I have Henri Geôlier's attention. "What do you mean?"

"When he gets out of gaol."

"He's already out of gaol. He got out two days ago."

"Where did he go?"

"I don't know. You'll have to ask him. If you can find him."

I request the prison records. I will add this information to my growing list of official documentation. Here it is in black ink on blue paper. Claude Thibault: incarcerated,

Friday, March 5, 1734; released Thursday, April 8, 1734.

Darkness has settled into the crevices by the time I get home. Madeleine has stew ready and waiting. It is hearty and hot and smells deliciously of spices and herbs. Everything else in town smells of smoke and rot and decay. The residue of fire.

We start with Madeleine's day. She bears the weight of the homeless, the bereft, the heartbroken. It is some consolation to remind ourselves that no one has died, but gloom is understandably everywhere.

So is uncertainty. People are looking for shelter, are looking to the kindness of family and friends. They are finding it, but conditions are not ideal. "The sisters slept outside in the garden last night. They will again tonight," Madeleine tells me.

I am shocked at the prospect that these women might have no where to go, no shelter from the cold and wet while the hospital and convent are rebuilt. "Surely someone will provide for the nuns of the Hôtel-Dieu."

"Someone has. Sister Cuillerier told me they will be staying in a house owned by Monsieur de Montigny."

I feel relief flood through me. This is good news. We need good news. "They must be pleased."

"They are grateful, certainly. But reality is stark. The house is big – one of the biggest in Montréal – but it was never intended to accommodate 40 people."

Madeleine understands my silence. Despair has crept into the crevices along with the darkness. She lets me brood. From somewhere a brandy appears. It is welcome.

"Let me tell you about my day."

Madeleine is delighted at my appointment as special rapporteur but understandably saddened by what has prompted this honour. "Is this why you were in the lower town? Why you are suddenly fascinated by wooden shingles?"

We laugh. It feels good. The seeds of happiness spring up from the belly and usher out our throats. We feel guilty almost instantly, but the guilt has a context and does not last. We forgive ourselves for being human.

"I was keeping busy with reports and archives and documents while waiting for Angélique to be arrested, for Rolant to tell me what was expected of me. When I ran out of paper to read, I went to rue Saint-Paul."

"Initiative is good even if the path does not lead to success."

"There are many paths to follow." I tell Madeleine about Claude Thibault, about the white man with a Black slave for a lover. She is not shocked.

"I saw him last night. With Angélique."

I sit up straight. "Where? When?"

"It was before the town crier accused her of arson. He was helping to move some of Madame de Francheville's possessions to the garden. But he did not help to fight the fire. I heard the hospital's gardener ask him why he was just standing there."

"What did he say?"

Madeleine smiles at my impatience. "He said he was tired."

It is, of course, not an acceptable answer, and I am surprised that Thibault would be so brazen. When I say this to Madeleine, she laughs softly. "You have this impression of slaves and servants as docile and deferential. I believe you will find this false as you walk the path of the special rapporteur."

My wife is right. There is much I will learn in the next few weeks that will shake my belief system and reshape my perceptions. "What else did you hear last night?"

"Everyone thinks she's guilty. Madame de Francheville accused her. The gardener accused her. Both of them did this even before Monsieur Roy made his way through the street and made the accusation public."

"What did Angélique say?"

"She said the same thing, every time to every accuser. 'I would not be so stupid.'"

"There is merit in that argument," I point out. "She lived in that house. Setting fire would make her homeless."

Madeleine tilts her head and looks at me with surprise and a little sadness. "You have not heard."

* * *

Marriage makes me happy. I did not know that it would. I worried the imposed togetherness, the repetition of the days with the same person would weigh on me, pull the joy from my heart over time. It has done the reverse. I am content. I am grateful. Marriage has made me happier.

To be precise, Madeleine has made me happier. I am aware of my good fortune. I am also aware that we have not been married long, less than a year. The brightest year of my life. I do not anticipate that will change. I do not think Madeleine would allow it.

I have learned gratitude from marriage. Certainly, I was grateful for many things before Madeleine, before our vows. Now I am grateful for so much more. Many of those things that sing to my heart are small things, like now. Madeleine has suggested we take a few minutes to look heavenward, to express our thankfulness that lives were spared yesterday. *God, was it only yesterday?*

We stand outside our home, hands clasped, silent. There is nothing at this moment to say, but there is much to feel. We

46

share those feelings without words. Words will come soon enough.

There is fresh coffee, refilled with a touch of brandy. Now there is conversation. This is husband and wife talking; this is also a witness speaking to the special rapporteur. We are aware of the line. We will not cross it.

Madeleine foregoes any preamble. "Angélique threatened Madame de Francheville. She said she would burn her house down."

I am shocked beyond words. That someone would say this. That a slave would say this. That a slave would do this. Madeleine can read my thoughts. "Remember, these are rumors. I am hearing these second and third hand from people who may have heard them second and third hand. This is not gospel."

I remind myself I am the special rapporteur. I am not here to take sides or to take information at face value. I write the word "rumeurs" at the top of the paper I have removed from my desk. I underline the word. "Tell me what you heard."

Madeleine has heard plenty. The first indication that Angélique threatened arson arose during a conversation between two women talking in the garden as the fire raged. Madeleine was making tea next to them. One of the women said Angélique had an argument with Madame de Francheville before her owner left for mass. Angélique warned her she would burn the house down.

The other woman, perhaps the Panis slave of Monsieur de Béréy, concurred. Angélique heard her mistress laughing and said she would not be laughing soon, she would not be sleeping in her own bed tonight.

"These were her words?" I am astonished at the temerity of the slave. Then I remind myself, again, I have misconceptions about slavery, and I have preconceived notions about Angélique's guilt that I must set aside.

Madeleine sips her coffee, cold now, but comforting nonetheless. "I do not think these are the only people who have heard Angélique threaten to burn down her owner's house. I got the sense from the people in the garden that Angélique has been angry for some time and Madame de Francheville has been the focus of that anger."

If my wife is correct, this may be a very short trial. Witnesses are a cornerstone of the French judicial system, a system that pits accusers and accused against each other to determine the truth. We do this without lawyers. We do not allow lawyers to practice in New France. We are not English.

"This is all second hand," my wife reminds me. "I did not hear Angélique say these things. I do not even know if these women heard Angélique say these things or are simply repeating what they have heard from others."

"We will sift fact from fiction," I assure my wife. "Judge Raimbault is fair and thorough."

"And yet," my wife points out between sips of cold coffee, "an arrest warrant was issued today based on nothing more than rumour."

That warrant was legal, allowed under the ordonnance criminelle of 1670. Introduced by King Louis XIV, the ordonnance codified criminal law in France, perhaps for the first time. It is an important tenet of our judicial system. I explain this to my wife.

"And yet," she says, pushing her coffee cup aside, "a woman is in jail because of rumours."

I make a note to review the ordonnance criminelle. I start to gather up our dishes. Something is nagging at the back of my mind. I kiss my wife, kiss the little one she embraces in her belly, and prepare for bed. The nagging persists.

By the time I wake up, after a fitful night, I know what I must find out. It is central to the case. *Why was Angélique so angry?*

Chapter 4
Accused
Monday, April 12, 1734

The courthouse is a beehive of activity. Marie-Joseph Angélique is being brought from her cell. I am at there when they bring her in. She carries her head high, and I wonder if she has learned this from her owner. But this is more than assurance, it is swagger. It is the full-frontal confidence of a defiant woman.

The men in the courtroom quietly look down on her. They will not rush to judgment even though French law says all accused are presumed guilty. Angélique must prove her innocence. At the helm are Judge Pierre Raimbault and François Foucher, our chief attorney.

Angélique is formally charged with arson. You can hear the silence reverberate in the room. This is a capital crime. The punishment: death, torture, or banishment. Or some combination of those. Being found guilty will mean an end to the life Angélique knows regardless of the punishment.

The typical questions are asked and answered. *What is your name? What is your age? Where do you live? How did you come to Montréal?*

There are other questions that must be uncomfortable for Angélique. Questions that will lead many to judgment. I do not believe this is the intent. Such questions must be asked. *Did you run away from your owner? Did you threaten to burn your owner's house to the ground?*

To the first question Angélique answers, "Yes." To the second question, she says, "No. I would have been possessed by the devil to have done so."

According to Angélique, when her owner accused her of arson, she said, "However nasty I might be, I am not wretched enough to do an act of that sort."

There were questions that surprised me, full of implication and information I have not uncovered. Judge Raimbault asks if Angélique pulled a young girl by her pinafore to stop her from yelling "Fire!"

Angélique sidesteps this question. She contends she did this to stop the girl and her friend Marguerite de Couagne from playing in the mud. I make a note to follow up on this line of questioning. It obviously has relevance for the judge.

Finally, Angélique admits she did go up to the roof of the house to feed the pigeons on the day of the fire, but to the surprise of everyone in the courtroom, she says, "I did not go alone. Madame de Francheville went with me."

An air of finality hangs in the room. There is one more question. It is obviously important. And I have no idea what it means. *On the night of the fire did you have a green blanket in your possession?*

* * *

The whole process does not take long. Angélique is escorted back to her cell. Those who sit in judgment rise and move on with their day. I head back to the corner I have created for myself at the back of the courtroom. I have with me the criminal ordinance of 1670 and other legal documents.

It does not take me long to find what I am looking for. Rumor alone constitutes legal grounds for accusing, arresting, and convicting an individual. I can feel Madeleine's disappointment before I even tell her. I am not sure I will. One thing I am sure of: things do not look good for Angélique.

It takes me several minutes to realize Angélique is not potentially alone in this crime. Alleged crime. There is the not-so-small-matter of Claude Thibault. There is a legal assumption that women are not responsible by nature and could be dominated by men. I am not sure I will tell Madeleine about this either. The assumption is premised on the contention that women involved in crimes are by their very nature

52

less culpable than the men they co-conspire with. The latter suspected of leading the former astray.

I make a note to ask Rolant about Thibault when we meet this afternoon. It is one of several questions I have on my list.

* * *

It is time for lunch. I have bread, cheese, dried fruit. In addition to sustenance, I need fresh air. I sit outside and try not to think about the mass of papers on my desk and the ruin of the lower town. Of course, it is all I think about.

At some point, I realize the courthouse has become a small hub of activity. Several merchants are arriving at rue Notre-Dame to record their losses. This is important. The official record given at the registry will protect them from lawsuits here at home or overseas in the homeland. I follow the first merchants into the registry. The first person I encounter is Pierre de Lestage. He speaks with the clerk. He relives the fire and identifies his losses: merchandise, documents, property. Others follow suit.

Many merchants will still be making an inventory of what has literally gone up in flames. This, in many cases, will be substantial. I will return tomorrow.

* * *

Rolant is waiting for me when I enter the courthouse. I apologize for my tardiness. He waves the apology away. "You are busy. It is as we would wish."

I feel myself warm with pleasure. I recount some of my efforts but underscore the preliminary nature of those efforts. "I have more questions than answers at this time. In particular, I wonder about Claude Thibault."

A small smile hovers at the corners of Rolant's mouth. "Aah, so you have gotten there." The warmth is back. "Thibault is a person of interest. It would appear he has escaped. No one can account for his whereabouts since the evening of the fire."

I nod. "That is the last account I also heard. Are the police looking for him?"

Now it is Rolant's turn to nod. "A manhunt is under way."

* * *

It may have been a slight exaggeration on my part to tell Rolant the "last account" I heard of Thibault agreed with his findings. I could more accurately have stated my "first and only account." I am embarrassed by my feint. I understand its impetus and wonder what I will do in the future when situations like this arise, as they undoubtedly will. Now this is something I will talk with Madeleine about.

In the meantime, I put the thought aside and make my way through the streets to rue Saint-Paul. I would like to speak with more people about the night of the fire, about Claude Thibault, about Angélique. I need to broaden my sphere if I am to be of true assistance as special rapporteur.

The street is much as it was yesterday. In ruins. Smoke still hangs heavy in the air. There is soot and grime everywhere. I will have to wash my boots tonight. Again. The garden for the poor is now a garden for everyone looking for a little respite. I half expect to see Madeleine here, but I do not. I do, however, see the servant girl who first ushered me into the de Béréy house. Sidonie.

I offer her a piece of fruit, leftover from my lunch. She takes it, gratefully I think, but I also know the sisters have been religiously feeding all who come here. I explain to Sidonie that I work with the court and that perhaps she could help me to understand what transpired on the night of April 10, or any time relevant to that night.

"I do not know anything, monsieur. I cannot help." Sidonie turns to walk away. The sense that she is smaller than when we first met returns to me. I regret having to push her, but I do.

"Perhaps you could tell me when you first saw the fire." I do not know where this question comes from or why I would want this information, but it stops Sidonie.

"I heard someone yell 'Fire!' before I saw flames or smelled smoke."

"Who was yelling?"

"I heard Angélique yell. I heard the children in the street yell. I ran outside. I was very much afraid."

"What did Angélique do?"

"I am told she ran next door to Monsieur Radisson's house, and he ran back with her. I heard him yell for a ladder, but I fear it was too late. You saw the fire, sieur, you know how it spread. Like the devil."

"What were you doing when the fire started?" I ask this not because I think Sidonie was somehow involved but I am trying to understand the sequence of events. Sidonie seems to understand my intent. She takes no offence.

"I was inside. I was on the main floor. I could hear Angélique yell clearly. I saw Marie-Manon outside. There was no one left in the house, so I went outside. I knew everyone could hear the screams."

"What did you do once you knew the flames were spreading?"

"I ran back into the house and grabbed what I could, what I thought would be of value or importance. I saw people with documents and furniture and clothes. I took what I could before the fire claimed the street."

"I'm sure the de Béréys are grateful. When you lose almost everything what remains becomes so much more important."

"It seemed like madness at the time, but as I look back now, there was an order to the madness. Everyone on the street was doing what I was doing. When we could do no more, we gathered in the garden."

"Did you see Angélique there?"

"I did. She did not seem upset. But she may have been. It cannot have been easy hearing everyone say you started the fire. They called her incendiaire to her face."

"I understand she did not back down."

"Angélique does not back down. Have you met her?"

"No," I acknowledge. "I only know her name."

"Everyone knows her name."

* * *

I record my conversation with Sidonie as I remember it. I try to reflect on what she said and how she said it. Accuracy is essential, and I am diligent in my efforts to achieve this. I know I am gathering information second hand, at least once removed from the source, who is imprisoned only a few dozen feet from where I now sit.

Sidonie asked if I had met Angélique. I have not. I will not. As special rapporteur, I work on the sidelines. I am not recording evidence; I am not interrogating the accused. But I have come to realize I play an important role in ensuring a fair and thorough trial. I must be painstaking with my research and my records.

I will go down paths that may to others seem unusual, even unnecessary. Certainly, less travelled. But this is my journey, and so I seek out, again, Henri Geôlier. He is, as before, in his private chamber. I wonder if he spends much of his day here. That is snide, I know, yet it is the thought that leaps to mind.

I bring fruit. That worked with Sidonie. It works again. "How goes the inquisicion?" Monsieur Geôlier asks between mouthfuls of dried apples. He laughs at his own joke.

I ignore the dig. "Slow but sure. I am hoping you can help."

This is a mistake. Monsieur Geôlier is not a man to volunteer assistance. I offer him more apples. *Thank you, Madeleine, for a very hearty lunch.*

"I know Angélique escaped once. I am trying to understand why."

"Why don't you ask her?" Monsieur Geôlier laughs at his own joke. Then he turns serious. "Did you read Thibault's arrest report?"

I am offended. Of course, I read the report. The jailer sees my reaction. Now I see his: surprise. "I would have thought it was in there."

"You would have thought what was in there?"

"The slave girl escaped so her owner could not sell her."

Henri Geôlier waits for my reaction. It is underwhelming. Turns out I needed more information. "To the West Indies."

Shock registers on my face and in my body. Monsieur Geôlier laughs. This is a good day for him.

* * *

Supper is sturgeon in a cream sauce. It is delicious, but my heart is not in it. Madeleine senses this despite my efforts to be present. There are preserves for dessert and coffee. I savour the aroma. I need pleasantries in my life today.

"Can you tell me?" Madeleine says this without rebuke or pressure. It is a simple question a wife has asked of her husband, and it deserves a simple answer.

"Yes." I recount my day, my questions of others, of myself.

"Do you think Angélique ran away because she feared being sold to the West Indies?"

"It would make me want to escape. Do you not agree?"

Madeleine hesitates. I am uncertain whether she is contemplating the question or formulating an answer that will not call my contention into question. "There is no doubt life as a slave in the Danish West Indies is a cruel life. I have heard the work is brutal, injuries are a constant, and there is disease. I would not want that life."

"And yet…"

A smile plays at my wife's lips. "And yet, I feel there may be more to this story. Let's take a walk."

We walk to the garden of the Hôtel-Dieu. I know we are here to seek out Sidonie, although I do not know why. "She may have more to offer," is all Madeleine says.

There are fewer people in the merchants' quarter than the night before. I suspect the numbers will dwindle over the next few days as the families find alternate accommodations. Sidonie told me the de Béréys already have a place to stay. I tell Madeleine this. "Sidonie will be here."

And she is. There is tea and bread making the rounds in the garden. People are eating and talking. There is even some laughter. The sisters are handing out blankets. Sidonie sees us and nods hello. We make our way to her. From somewhere in the folds of her frock, Madeleine offers Sidonie some preserves from our dessert. The servant girl takes them appreciatively.

We sit on a bench at the edge of the garden, away from other ears but not too far away to attract attention. "My husband is trying to understand why Angélique would have run away. We're hoping you can help."

"I do not know why she ran away."

"But you have a guess, eh?" I am impressed, as always, at my wife's acumen. "We were told she had been sold to the West Indies."

There is a spark in Sidonie's eyes. She knows something we do not. This has value in her world, and ours. "Angélique was sold to Monsieur Cugnet. He is a very important man." Sidonie says this without emotion, but there is a breathlessness to the statement. I am uncertain if this is excitement or alarm, or both.

The pronouncement certainly has some shock value. François-Étienne Cugnet is a member of the Conseil Supérieur, the high court. He is also a businessman, a partner in the Saint-Maurice Ironworks. I agree with Sidonie. This is an important man – who lives in the city of Québec, not the West Indies.

"She did not want to live with Monsieur Cugnet?" Madeleine asks bringing me back to the conversation.

"It is said he was going to sell her to the West Indies as soon as Madame de Francheville could get a ship to take Angélique from Montréal to Québec. She did not have much time. The river is thawing already."

It is as if we feel, here in this garden, the pressure Angélique must have felt as she watched the ice melt and her life slip further away from her. "They say Angélique begged her mistress not to sell her. Then she threatened to burn the house down."

"That did not have any effect?" I ask.

"No," says Sidonie. "Madame de Francheville got 600 pounds of gunpowder for Angélique. That is worth a lot of money."

"But there is more …." Madeleine prompts Sidonie.

"Madame de Francheville was afraid. Angélique was brazen. She talked back, she warned she would do bad things, she acted out. One servant quit because of her. Madame de Francheville did not want to be alone in the house with Angélique." The breathlessness is back.

The sisters arrive with tea. We thank them and sip our beverage slowly. I appreciate what Sidonie has told me. I do not see its relevance at this moment, but the fuller the picture I am able to paint the more helpful I will be.

"Do you think she loved him?" My wife's question comes out of nowhere. It takes me a few seconds to understand what she is asking. It does not take Sidonie that long.

The servant girl stiffens, then shrugs. "Perhaps. Perhaps not. Thibault was not her first lover. She had three children with another Black slave. The children did not live. Maybe Thibault gave her what her other lover couldn't – a chance at freedom. It is easier to travel with a white man, is it not?"

***

April 12, 1734

Cher Maman, Papa,

There is so much to tell you. Little is good. Two days ago, Montréal burned. And burned. A fire started in the lower town, where the merchants live and do business, where the hospital for the poor and ill resides. By the next day, forty-five homes were rendered to ash. The convent/hospital was gone. Again. Fortunately, no one died. We have said prayers of thanks for that blessing.

Smoke hangs heavy in the air. So does recrimination. A Black slave, Marie-Joseph Angélique, is accused of arson. The town crier heralded the accusation the night of the fire. The next day she was arrested. Justice is swift in Montréal.

It is also cautious. To ensure justice is done and not merely service with the lips only, I have been appointed special rapporteur. This is an honour. It brings me, and Madeleine, much joy. But we are saddened it comes from the ashes of tragedy. Literally.

I am expected to speak to those who are not likely to be called as witnesses, to review court documents and laws, confirm witness statements, ensure there is even greater diligence in the process of arriving at a verdict in this case.

I have already started. Much of this work is familiar territory. I review documents. I make notes. I raise questions and seek out answers. Much is unfamiliar though. I realize most of my work as a court reporter has been as observer and recorder of what I saw and heard. I have not been in the role of questioner before. I do not know that I like it, but I will do my very best. Justice deserves no less, nor does my superior, Rolant. He is a man of integrity.

It is in my role as questioner that I have an inquiry of you, Papa. Wooden shingles. We believe this is where the fire started and why it spread so quickly. For reasons I cannot explain, I have removed three shingles from the street. I wonder if they have anything to say about the nature of the fire. I found these shingles not where expected, perhaps. They are distinctly blackened. This may be nothing. If perchance, it is, I turn to you for any insight.

It is not just shingles that have me perplexed. The world here is so different from our world, from Acadie. I do not know if that is because I paint a naïve picture of my home or if the distinctions are truly marked.

Slaves here do housework, they care for children, some toil in the fur trade. They are an inherent part of the economy and the fabric of life, but the threads they weave are invisible to most of us. We do not see them; we simply accept that they are there.

Such acceptance does not come easily to some of them. The things Angélique said to her owner are shocking. This made for a relationship of fear and resentment, I believe. It is part of my job to find out.

Now it is time for bed. Madeleine and the little one are already asleep. I will join them and dream of Acadie.

Your loving son,
Philippe

PS The herbs you sent have worked wonders. Madeleine can keep food down and feels much better.

Chapter 5
Accused
Tuesday, April 13, 1734

Two words appear to be on everyone's lips: arson and Angélique. It is not surprising. The town lies in ruins, an unapologetic slave accused of levelling it. No other subject could possibly be as significant, as timely, or as dramatic. Despite the buzzing that permeates the streets and the courthouse, I know it will be several weeks before the trial begins, before Angélique's accusers have their day in court, and she ultimately gets to confront them.

In the meantime, I learn more about Angélique. I delve into registry materials and other documentation I have access to here. A picture of the slave's life begins to emerge. She is 29 years old, born in 1705 in Madeira, Portugal. She is a long way from home.

I am not able to piece together much of her early life, records likely residing in Portugal, if they even exist. What is well known is that her native country started the Atlantic slave trade almost two centuries ago bringing men, women, and children from Africa to Europe and elsewhere. Slavery is an economic mainstay for Portugal.

It may well be that Angélique was first enslaved in the country in which she was born. There are records of her sale as a teenager to Nichus Block, a Flemish merchant. He, in turn, sold her to François Poulin de Francheville in 1725 although she did not arrive in Montréal via Europe. Monsieur de Francheville purchased her in New England. That would likely be easy enough for a man in the fur trade.

I try to imagine what it must be like to barter for human life. I fail. I am relieved I fail.

*　*　*

Lunch is a welcome respite from eye strain and human anguish. There is hopelessness in these documents spread out before me, and I am relieved to turn my attention to cold ham, bread, and fruit. Three bites in, Henri Geôlier shows up at my desk.

"Aah, here you are. I have been looking for you."

It is impressive how the jailer manages to locate me when I have food in front of me. I offer him bread and ham. He helps himself. Tomorrow, I decide, I will go home and have lunch with Madeleine.

"Is there a problem?" I know the answer before I ask the question, but I am hopeful we can be done with our conversation while there is still food left.

"Just the opposite," Monsieur Geôlier says between mouthfuls of ham. "It occurred to me you might not know Angélique asked for congé."

I sit up, food forgotten. This is significant, another reason why Angélique may have escaped and why she would want to burn her mistress's home to the ground. In the simplest of terms, "congé" means "leave." In a world of slavery, it means "freedom."

"December." So, she asked Madame de Francheville to release her from bondage before she ran away. I am assuming her owner denied the request.

"How do you know?" Before I consider the implications of this information, I need to ensure it is accurate.

"Everyone who has been within five feet of Angélique knows this. Have you not met her?" Monsieur Geôlier stares at me with that look of superiority, the one he wears like a permanent scar. "Aah, that's right. You have not met her."

The jailer doesn't even try to hide his grin. It doesn't matter. I can confirm this information with Sidonie. Monsieur Geôlier stands to leave. First though he pops the final piece of ham in his mouth.

* * *

Sidonie is sifting aimlessly through the rubble that is now the merchants' quarter when I arrive in the lower town. She looks like she has not been sleeping. She stops when she sees me. "There is nothing to find. Yet we look." I realize Sidonie is not alone. Other servants and slaves are in the quarter combing for something salvageable.

"I wanted to ask you a question, but I don't want to interrupt your work."

"It is time for tea," says Sidonie. We head to the garden, to the pot of hot water that is always at the ready.

I ask about congé. Sidonie looks away, somewhere in the distance. "It was not a happy time. Madame de Francheville told her 'no.'" She leans in. "Angélique was not happy. She yelled at her mistress. She called her a whore."

Surprise is written across my face. Surely not. As if reading words of disbelief etched on my skin, Sidonie nods. "She made life miserable for everyone. Madame de Francheville should have let her go." Sidonie is back looking into the distance. "But 600 pounds of gunpowder is a lot of money."

"What did Madame de Francheville do when Angélique yelled at her? Threatened her?" I ask, in part, because I do not know what I would do.

"Madame would whip Angélique although less recently, less since her husband died." Sidonie takes a sip of tea, and a breath. "It is funny, eh, the woman who can whip the slave is afraid of the slave."

* * *

I return to the courthouse to review my notes and to add to them what I learned from Sidonie. Perhaps I will also seek out Rolant, update him on progress. But really there is no progress. We are in a state of limbo until the trial begins and witness testimony is given. That is unless I am asked to sit in on the investigation directly. I have not been asked so far, and I suspect this is not the role of special rapporteur. This is the role of the King's counsellor, François Foucher. He does not strike me as a man who asks for help or needs it. My job is to stay more in the shadows than the light.

I no sooner think of Sieur Foucher then he walks through the courthouse doors. He appears to be in a hurry, determined. He heads toward the registry. Without really knowing why I follow him. In the shadows.

He is speaking with the clerk about losses incurred during the fire. It is a complex situation involving a mortgage of 3,328 livres, 15 sols, and 8 deniers owed by Nicolas Perthuis and his wife. Their house is now burned to the ground. In addition, Sieur Foucher also lost two credit notes, one for approximately 700 livres and the other for about 200 livres. It is a lot of money. For many, it is a lifetime of earnings.

The exchange hits home. I have been thinking of the fire and the devastation it has wrought on people's homes, goods,

70

belongings. Sieur Foucher has reminded me that business, legal and commercial, has been affected significantly as well. Nothing burns as quickly as paper. Commerce and the law exist primarily on paper.

Sieur Foucher is straddling two worlds: government and commerce. It will be difficult to investigate the slave who burned your business to the ground even if your own home is still standing in another part of town. I am reminded, again, of the importance of the role I play from the shadows.

* * *

Sieur Foucher's visit to the Royal Registry has me pondering loss. Certainly, men (and some women) lost business assets in the fire. Property burned to ash and with it the enterprises that operated inside those walls were destroyed. But loss is more than things, of course, it is treasured possessions, it is mementos of loved ones, it is the memory of safety and comfort.

Some have lost more than others, perhaps no one more so than Madame de Francheville. I am not sure why, but I spend the afternoon with documents that help me understand her life – and her losses. Foremost among those, what is called a mutual donation.

I pack up the papers and put my thoughts in the desk with them. It is time to

71

walk home, to think about spring, and flowers. New growth and sunshine. Death can wait until tomorrow.

Or at least until a hot cup of tea.

* * *

Madeleine is always interested in my day. My job is a source of conversation and, more importantly, connection. She has insights I do not bring to my work but that enhance that work. That was never more true than now. Madeleine has lived through this fire as I have, but not like I have. She has spoken with people I have yet to meet. She has spoken with people I have met, but differently. Still, I do not want to impose; I do not want to take advantage. My wife feels the same. So, we wait until tea to talk about what we really want to talk about.

"I have learned much about Angélique's life today. It is, perhaps, as one would expect. It is also most unexpected."

"What surprised you?" my wife asks. I am prepared with an answer and findings from documents that made me sit back in my chair for reasons I do not fully understand.

"There are facts tossed into court records like dried orange peel in our tea. They give flavour to a life but are often submerged."

"Such as?"

"Would you be surprised to learn Angélique was baptized."

"I would not." My wife smiles suspecting, perhaps, I am leading her down a path that will, ultimately, surprise her. "We are Catholic. We are baptized. Angélique lived and worked in a Catholic household. Madame de Francheville is a devout woman."

"Angélique was purchased by the de Franchevilles nine years ago. She was baptized four years ago." My wife sits back, surprise etched on her face.

"That is a long time to wait. That is a long time to go without a Christian name."

"It is the law. It is in the Code noir." I do not need to explain this legal decree to my wife. It is well known, certainly among those in the legal sphere and those who own slaves. I suspect it is commonly known to the townsfolk even if it does not touch their lives. The Code explicitly states how slaves are to be treated in New France. It discusses punishment and freedom of movement, or more accurately, lack of movement. The Code also requires all slaves convert to Catholicism. It is an owner's responsibility to ensure this happens. Sooner rather than later.

"Why would Monsieur de Francheville wait so long?"

"Perhaps Angélique was already baptized. She was born in Portugal. Perhaps she kicked up a fuss. We know she has a wicked tongue."

"Do you think it matters?"

That is the question I have been asking myself again and again. I know the answer. "It will if she is sentenced to die."

Chapter 6
Accused
Wednesday, April 14, 1734

Today I will focus on the de Franchevilles. Madame will play a key role in the trial. She accused Angélique of arson shortly after the fire started and before the town crier made the accusation public. There is a reason for her assurance, and it will come out in her testimony although it is clear this belief about Angélique's guilt and Madame's animosity are rooted in the relationship between owner and slave.

I would like to know more about that relationship, and I will start by learning more about the slave owner. As always, there are many documents to help me in my quest.

Thérèse de Couagne was born on January 19, 1697, in Montréal. *This is her home. She belongs here.* I wonder if that makes the loss of her house now all the more heart wrenching. As I read, I discover Madame de Francheville has suffered more losses in her life than wood and stone.

The first great loss was likely her father, Charles de Couagne, who died in 1706. Thérèse de Couagne would only have been nine years old, a child. Admittedly, a child of wealth. Charles de Couagne had been one of the richest merchants in Montréal. His daughter would have grown up in the lap of luxury, and in 1718, when she was twenty-one, she married François Poulin de Francheville an ambitious young merchant. Her dowry was 2,500 livres.

They would be married for fifteen years. The ambitious young merchant Thérèse de Couagne wed was a very wealthy man in his own right when he died in 1733. I check the death records. No cause of death is given, but we have been ravaged by pox in New France. No one is immune.

I am sure her husband's death devastated Madame de Francheville, but as I read through the records of her life I wonder if there wasn't a greater devastation. The de Franchevilles had a child. The child died after only a few weeks. I sit and stare at the record of death. I know, in part, this numbness I feel is because I am about to become a father. Madeleine will shortly give birth. I continue to stare at the record of death.

The child's name was Marie-Angélique.

* * *

Madeleine is surprised to see me. I am surprised to be here. I do not usually come home during the day. Today, the sun was shining, and I needed a walk. I have brought my lunch with me. Madeleine puts on a pot of water. She takes my hand.

"Let us talk of happy things."

I return to work full, content.

* * *

Rolant is waiting for me. He waves away my protestations. "You are doing your job. I do not need a detailed list of where you go or why." I like this man.

What he has to say next is less satisfying. "The bailiffs have had no luck finding Claude Thibault." He hands me a written deposition.

Over the last two days, two bailiffs attempted to apprehend Thibault at the residence of Dame Portneuf. They were told he had not returned there and were directed to the home of a local merchant. The merchant's son said he did not know Thibault. The bailiffs persisted, visiting a residence where a former servant of Madame de Francheville lives. She said she had not seen the man since he left gaol. The bailiffs even followed up on rumours Thibault was travelling on the Chemin de la Coste St. Joseph. No luck.

"We are hunting a man who refuses to be found." Rolant's frustration is palpable.

"How can I help?"

"You have been out talking to people. People who know Thibault. Is there anyone who could help?"

I think of Sidonie. "There is a woman, a servant in the neighbourhood. I can ask her. She has been helpful."

"Bien. We can use all the help we can get."

* * *

I head to the merchants' quarter, but Sidonie is not there. I see the Panis slave Marie-Manon, but she scurries away as I approach. I will have to come back this evening to see if Sidonie has returned. In the meantime, I have paperwork.

The early afternoon chafes. I read about François Poulin de Francheville's rise through the ranks of commerce. He was more than a man of ambition. He had vision. His most recent vision it would appear was ironclad. He had received the Crown's official blessing to mine iron ore found at Saint-Maurice. That blessing was extended for twenty years.

Monsieur de Francheville would not live to see the project through to the end. But his wife well may. The couple had signed a contract, often called a "gift," that would protect each other financially. The gift ensured that should Monsieur de Francheville die his possessions would become his wife's possessions, and vice versa. The greatest protection though would have been afforded to Madame de

Francheville. *He must have loved her very much.*

At her husband's death, Madame de Francheville received the house on rue Saint-Paul and a farm in Saint-Michel. There was also his business including the iron ore company. She will never have to worry about money, I think. Then I realize that was the least of her worries.

* * *

Madeleine and I head to the lower town after supper in search of Sidonie. It is as if she is waiting for us. We have brought food; this has become our routine. I hope though that Sidonie is not in need of nutrition. I feel confident she is well fed and taken care of, but I realize I do not know what this confidence is founded on.

We sip tea and talk about the restoration, such as it is. Many homeowners are already beginning the process of cleaning up and rebuilding. Sidonie tells us Madame de Francheville is one of them despite everything that is going on. I ask what she means. *Everything that is going on.*

"The trial looms. Madame de Francheville met with the judge and the prosecutor today."

I sit up straight. This is news to me, as it would be. Judge Raimbault and Monsieur Foucher, the chief attorney, do not inform me of their plans to depose witnesses. Rolant should have known though.

"Do you know if it went well?" I do not know what I mean by "well," but I would like as much information as possible and want to keep the conversation going.

"I have heard it was brief. Madame said what happened. The judge and the procureur listened. Someone wrote it down. Then it was over."

That makes sense. The investigation is preliminary. "Do you know what she said?"

"What she has said all along. Angélique is guilty. She started the fire."

"Do you think she is guilty?" Madeleine asks. The question seems to throw Sidonie off stride.

"I would not know, Madame. I was not there where the fire started."

"But you do know Angélique," Madeleine pointed out.

"I do not want to accuse her when I do not know. There are enough people doing that already."

This was not the answer I had expected. Sidonie is perhaps the first person to put into words what has been rolling around in my head: no one saw Angélique start the fire, at least as far as I can ascertain. *Will we burn a woman to death based on words others heard others say?*

"You are right," I say to Sidonie. "But it is helpful always to have insight and understanding. You never know what will be helpful when you are trying to be just."

"What is it you want to know?" So, I am not as clever as I think.

"We're looking for Claude Thibault. Have you seen him?"

"Not since the night of the fire."

"Have you heard anything about where he might be?" This is Madeleine. I am glad she asked the question. It sounds less authoritative, less official. Acquaintances chatting over tea.

"The police are looking for him. We all know that. They are even asking some servants." So, not an answer to the question.

"We're thinking someone may be hiding him. Someone perhaps who believes he is innocent."

Sidonie looks at me as if reading between the lines of my face. "Who would be so foolhardy? If the police found out ...."

I can hear the fear in Sidonie's voice. It is a good point. Someone would have to be very brave or very foolish to do this.

"Do you think he loves Angélique? Do you think she loves him?" The question surprises both Sidonie and me.

Sidonie dismisses the idea with a wave of her hand. "This is not love. Convenience maybe. They escaped together."

Madeleine pushes back in that gentle way she has of letting you know she will persist until she gets what she wants. "That would be good for Angélique. Surely, though, it would be harder for Thibault to travel with a Black woman. They would stand out."

"Perhaps they were lovers," Sidonie concedes. "I doubt they were ever in love." The servant girl leans in. "I will tell you this. Everyone says he is gone from here, from Montréal. That would be the safest."

It would indeed. But who wants Claude Thibault to be safe?

* * *

We're dodging mud, unsuccessfully. Heading home. Both preoccupied with our conversation with Sidonie and the treachery that are the streets of Montréal in April. Madeleine is tired. I realize I am as well.

I feed the fire when we get home and make us both a hot chocolate. We deserve the treat, the warmth.

"Was that helpful?"

"I did not know about the deposition. Tomorrow will be busy. I will be glad to have things in writing."

"You are more comfortable when things are in writing."

My wife knows me well. There is a finality and a definitiveness to the written word. I am at home in this world.

"Did you learn what you wanted to learn about Claude Thibault?"

"I did not learn where he was. I did not expect to, but one can dream."

82

Madeleine caresses my arm. She is beginning to drift off to sleep. Her eyelids are heavy. "But you did learn something important about Sidonie."

Chapter 7
Testimony
Thursday, April 15, 1734

The bell for prime rings out as I head down rue Saint-Antoine. I picture the sisters making their way to the first daylight service as I make my way to the courthouse under the rays of a weak but hopeful sun. The sisters will kneel before God; I will immerse myself once more in paper. We are both praying for the same thing.

I am early. Rolant is earlier. The senior court reporter is waiting for me. He can tell by the look on my face I am not surprised to see him. This thought, it appears, pleases him.

"You know."

"I heard last night. From the servant girl."

"So, it is being discussed."

"I would dare to surmise it is the only topic of discussion in many homes."

Rolant smiles, at my humor or the truth of the statement I am not sure. "Tell me first what you found out."

"Sidonie says she has not seen Claude Thibault, that no one would be foolish enough to harbour him."

"Do you believe her?"

"I believe she is telling me what she wants me to know. I also believe there is more she is not telling me. Yet."

"Do you think she knows where he is?"

"I did not get that impression. She did say she heard he had left town. I do not know whether she knows this first hand or second hand, but it makes sense. If a man is fleeing, you do not remain in the town you need to escape."

"Do you think this woman would know what she speaks of?"

"She knows Angélique. She knows Thibault. She is surrounded by those who live on rue Saint-Paul. She certainly hears things."

"I will tell the bailiffs, but I suspect there is little they can do at this stage. We will have to wait for our clever little fur trader to slip up."

* * *

For the next few minutes, we talk dispositions. Over the last two days, five people have been deposed; another seven are scheduled for this afternoon. Rolant has received permission for me to sit in on the depositions. In the shadows.

This gives me the morning to review yesterday's testimony and to start to paint a picture of the events of April 10.

The trial has begun.

Étienne Volant Radisson

A sixty-nine-year-old colonel in the militia, Étienne Volant Radisson was the first witness. I can hear the confidence and outrage in Radisson's voice as I read the transcript. I put a star by this note. I may be reading a familial tone into the words that is not intended. Sieur Radisson is a first cousin to François Poulin de Francheville.

I write my own summary, putting words in his mouth as I understand them from the court report. "I returned from prayer. It was about seven o'clock. The Black slave came to me. She said there was a fire at her home. I grabbed two pails of water."

Monsieur Radisson said floorboards were on fire in the attic. They were under the rooftop. Angélique was screaming, "Aah, my Lord, the fire is everywhere." She ran downstairs.

What Sieur de Francheville's first cousin did not see anywhere was a ladder he could use to get to the attic. He did what many in the neighbourhood did: ran to save what he could from his own home.

Monsieur Radisson continued his testimony. He noted that he has since heard, admittedly third hand, that Madame de Béréy's servant told her Angélique had said earlier that evening of her mistress, "That bitch will not laugh so much later. She will not sleep in her house."

The servant is not Sidonie. Of that, I am convinced. I wonder if "servant" should be "slave." If this is Marie-Manon who is being quoted.

I also wonder what I have learned from this. I take a moment to reflect. Two things, I conclude. First, Angélique ran for help. Second, it was too late.

Thérèse de Couagne de Francheville

Madame de Francheville was the second witness. She started off on what I felt was a pivotal note: *I do not know who set the fire in my house.*

The thirty-six-year-old widow, as she is described in the deposition, said she knew Angélique had gone to the attic the day before the fire started but was not aware she had been upstairs on the day of the fire. I make a note: *This contradicts Angélique's testimony.*

Also, on the day before the fire, April 9th, Claude Thibault came to visit Madame de Francheville. He wanted to be paid. I imagine this was not a pleasant conversation. Something undoubtedly got under Madame de Francheville's skin. She told Thibault she had sold Angélique. She told him this in no uncertain terms. "I do not want to keep her. I do not want her in my home." Madame de Francheville also said she thought sharing these thoughts with

Claude Thibault may have been imprudent. I agree.

It was not only Angélique Madame de Francheville wanted out of her house. She told the indentured servant she did not want him there either. It was a request, or a demand, that went unheeded. We know Claude Thibault was there on the night of April 10 helping to remove some of the belongings from the house to the Hôtel-Dieu.

Marguerite de Couagne

This person is new to me. She is one of the two children who were playing outside when the fire started. Now she has a name.

Ten-year-old Marguerite is Madame de Francheville's niece. The child is an interesting witness. She has nothing new to add to the testimony. She says she does not know who set the fire (this seems to be a growing theme), but she affirms she has heard about the threats others have said Angélique made. Little Marguerite said shortly before the fire started she saw Angélique pouting in the kitchen then head out the door to speak to the Panis slave next door. Marguerite has since heard it said that Angélique told the slave girl Madame de Francheville would not sleep in her house that night. Stating that was all she knew, Marguerite then went on to say that she had previously seen Claude Thibault and Angélique in the kitchen together.

Marie dit Manon

The deposition records the Panis slave's name as Marie, called Manon. I have only heard her called Marie-Manon. The record says she is fifteen, or "thereabouts." The girl is a central witness. There is no hearsay here.

Marie-Manon told the court that shortly before the fire she was sitting in front of her owner's house when Angélique dropped by. It sounded like a friendly visit: *She came to tickle me, to make me laugh.* I feel some relief that there may be laughter in Marie-Manon's life. I remember the stare she gave me, more accurately through me, the first time we saw each other. At least, the first time I saw her.

What Marie-Manon says next is not good news for Angélique: Madame de Francheville's slave returned home only to come right back. Her mistress was laughing with a neighbour, Madame Desrivières. Angélique told Marie-Manon her owner "will not long be in her home and will not sleep there."

There's more. Marie-Manon said Angélique returned home, but she saw her three or four times come into the street and look toward the roof. Fifteen minutes later someone shouted "Fire!" Marie-Manon left the de Béréy home, her home, and saw the pigeonhole on the roof of the de Francheville house was ablaze.

Marie-Manon then did what perhaps any slave would do, at least would be expected to do. She told her owner what Angélique had said.

Charlotte Trottier Desrivières

There is one final witness: Charlotte Trottier Desrivières. The ten-year-old playmate of Marguerite de Couagne had nothing to add – and something to add. She said she saw Angélique in the kitchen before the fire started, then she heard someone going up the stairs of the de Francheville home. Another young girl said this was Angélique climbing the stairs.

All that is certain: when the fire was first seen Angélique was on the doorstep in plain sight.

* * *

It is time for lunch. As if on cue, Henri Geôlier appears. Monsieur Geôlier's visits have become an almost daily occurrence and always at lunch. The former surprises me; the latter does not. I'm having a simple repast: bread and eggs. I notice Madeleine has put extra eggs in my midday meal. The jailer helps himself.

"Things are moving, eh?"

Of course, Monsieur Geôlier would know what is happening given where he lives and works. There is the small courtroom off the prison where I have my desk. If testimony is presented here, he will be with easy earshot. And he has ongoing access to Angélique. I envy him that access, but I wonder what any of us would really learn from this woman that she did not want us to know.

"What have you heard?" There is no pretense anymore. Monsieur Geôlier knows I want his information; I know he wants my food.

* * *

"It does not look good for the slave."

This much I already know. Still... "Why do you say that?"

The jailer looks at me as if I have just grown a second head. He does not bother to answer the question. "The slave is doing well."

I offer Monsieur Geôlier another egg. "Why do you say that?"

The distain is back. "Because I see her, and I hear her everyday. She contends she is innocent. It is endless. To anyone who will listen."

"Do you think she is innocent?"

"I do not think it is up to me to decide. The court will do that. I trust the court. She will be found guilty."

So much for objectivity. I regret having given away my last hardboiled egg.

Monsieur Geôlier leans in as if we are about to share a confidence. "Judge Raimbault will take no chances. I hear the notaries talking. They say more than twenty witnesses will be called. They will be called more than once. No chance for error here."

I am impressed. This is expansive; indeed, this may well be the most extensive trial to ever take place in New France. A Black woman accused of arson. A slave accused of betraying her mistress. Voltaire could create a masterful play from the flames that have devastated Montréal. I wonder if it would be a tragedy.

The jailer is not a man prone to reflection. Lunch is gone, and he rises to take his leave. He pushes his chair back into the table, an unusual move (it is generally left there for me to align). This may be an opportunity. There is a question that is bothering me. Monsieur Geôlier may have some insight.

"The police have not found Claude Thibault. They have looked and looked."

I am stating the obvious. Usually, Monsieur Geôlier would dismiss this foolishness with a wave of his hand. He looks at me. "What is it you want to know?"

I underestimate the jailer. "Could it be that someone would hide the man. Would anybody be so reckless?"

"You know the answer to that question." Monsieur Geôlier looks at me carefully. I blush under the scrutiny. "Why do you not want to admit the answer?"

* * *

I make my way to the depositions. I feel myself hurrying. This is dread. And excitement. Trials in New France are dramatic. There is a legal presumption of guilt, and the onus is on the accused to prove their innocence. I am wondering how Angélique will do this. If she can do this.

First, though, the tribunal – the judge, the prosecutor, and the court reporter – must prepare for the case. The first step, where we are today, involves witness testimony. Soon Angélique will be able to confront her accusers but not today. Today the case against her will unfold.

Jacques-Hippolyte Leber de Senneville

We start today where we ended yesterday: with the testimony of a child. The boy is older, fifteen, son of Sieur de Senneville, a navy lieutenant. He watched his grandmother's house go up in flames. Like almost everyone who came before him, the young man says he did not know who set the fire, but he heard from the Panis slave that Angélique said her mistress would not sleep in her house tonight.

The consistency of the hearsay is noteworthy. It is also noteworthy that the trial to date, for the most part, has been nothing more than hearsay. That is legally enough to convict. I am not sure it will satisfy Judge Raimbault. It is my fervent hope it will not.

I am about to discover that concern may not matter.

Marguerite César dit Lagardelette

The seventh witness is a neighbour of Madame de Francheville. The woman, roughly fifty-two years of age, says shortly before the fire she was looking out her window and saw the Black slave in front of the de Francheville home. According to Madame César, Angélique looked worried. She glanced from side to side, she locked eyes with Madame César, she looked toward the Hôtel-Dieu, she went back into the house but quickly came outside again.

It was strange behaviour, thought Madame César. So strange, in fact, the neighbour woman left her perch at the window and went outdoors to find out why Angélique was acting this way. She was unable to discover what was making the slave behave strangely. Madame César could see nothing in the street to account for Angélique's unusual actions, and the whole thing tired the neighbour out. She returned home, not feeling well. She had barely sat down when the cry of "Fire!" was heard.

Madame César ended her testimony on what I'm sure she thought was the definitive pronouncement. *I know the Negress to be bad.*

I also know Madame César to be savvy. At the end of her testimony, she requested payment. The court awarded her thirty sols.

* * *

Madame César's testimony has transformed the energy in the room. I can feel it. As I look around, I sense that the tribunal feels it too. There are nods. I swear I even saw at least one man smile although that was quickly stifled. This is not a convivial matter.

The neighbour woman has offered up firsthand testimony of Angélique's behaviour on the night of the fire. Indeed, Madame César found that behaviour so troublesome she left her home to see for herself what was happening on the street. The answer, she said without hesitation, was nothing.

The implication is clear: if there was nothing outside to spark the unusual behaviour it had to be something inside, something only Angélique knew.

We are only two witnesses into the afternoon. I suspect more surprises are in store.

The forty-one-year-old wife of Sieur Jean de Latour, well-regarded in the merchants' quarter, brings us back to unfounded information and supposition. She did not see Angélique set the fire. We will have to acknowledge at some point that no one did. I wonder how this might affect the outcome of the trial.

Despite a complete lack of evidence, and with nothing more than conviction, Madame de la Baume says that when she saw the fire, she knew it was Angélique who had set it. So convinced was she of the truthfulness of her belief she shared it with Sieur Radisson. Further fueling her conviction were comments she had heard children say about Angélique and her mistress. *She said she would burn her. She would cut her throat.*

Madame de la Baume also states that Marie-Louise Poirier, the servant who left Madame de Francheville because of Angélique, told her that the slave's hatred extended beyond her mistress. *She said if she returned to her country and found any Frenchmen there, she would have them all perish.*

* * *

I find Madame de la Baume's testimony compelling, not so much for its content but for the conviction I hear in her voice. There is no doubt this woman believes what she is saying, so much so she sought out someone on the night of the fire to share her fears. This, of course, does not make it so. Indeed, it makes it much more of the same. The court will recognize this, but will they wane under the repetition? How often can we be told that we heard someone say something threatening without believing the threats to be real after a while? How often can we be told someone was accused of a crime without becoming convinced they committed the crime?

And this is only the second day of testimony.

Marie-Louise Poirier

The trial reminds me that New France can be a harsh place to live. Our ninth witness is Madame de Francheville's former servant. Marie-Louise Poirier is twenty-eight years old, and she is a widow. She is also not a fan of Angélique. A little over a week before the fire, the former servant says she stopped Angélique from imbibing eau de vie and leaving the house without permission. In response, Angélique threatened her with bodily harm.

I make a mental note to ask Sidonie about jobs for servants. Are they plentiful? Would a servant leave a good job without there being a very serious reason?

It would appear Poirier was a valued member of the household. Thérèse de Francheville informed her departing servant she would be welcome back, and sooner rather than later. She was selling Angélique, and when the barges began flowing downstream for Québec that spring, Marie-Louise could return.

This confirms earlier testimony regarding the sale of Angélique. Poirier also confirms the hatred that seems to define much of Angélique's life. *She many times stated that if she ever reached her country and there were whites there, she would see them burned like dogs. They are without worth.*

The former servant also has new information about Angélique and the fire. She testifies that when Angélique fled with Claude Thibault she stole three deer skins. As to the fire itself, Poirier says when she was returning from prayer, she saw flames coming through the roof. There were no flames in the chimney.

The court thanked Poirier and honoured her request for payment: fifteen sols.

* * *

Three more witnesses follow. I try to keep a mental tally of where there is consistency among the accounts and where there are points of difference. Marie-Josèphe Bizet offers the latter. Before the fire started, she saw Angélique. The slave appeared to be calm and in good humour. Admittedly, this was well before the fire started.

Jean Joseph Laflamendiere came next. The forty-one-year-old surgeon says he saw Angélique drinking with two men he did not know the night of the fire. He accused her of drinking fruit brandy. She said it was syrup and proved it by giving him a taste. Still, he went to warn the sisters there might be an issue. By the time they returned, Angélique was alone.

* * *

A lethargy fills the courtroom. I am not sure if this is a general weariness or a physical response to hearing the same thing over and over, but nuanced. How to separate the minutiae from the meat of the testimony? How to avoid the danger in doing that?

The final witness does not have much to say, but she leaves us with much to think about. Françoise Geoffrion, a widow and servant, tells the court she met Angélique early on the afternoon of the fire. The twenty-two-year-old asked Angélique if she was having a quiet stroll and still with Madame de Francheville. The slave told her she had little time to stroll and that she would not be living with her mistress for much longer.

* * *

The lethargy I felt in the courtroom I feel in my bones as I rise to leave. I need to make notes, to put my thoughts on paper. I do not know if I have the energy. I decide to wait until tomorrow to read the written depositions. This will give me the evening to think and, if I am fortunate, to not think.

* * *

We walk arm in arm. Breathing in the night air, solaced by candle flames flickering in windows. Madeleine is tired. The baby has been busy today. I share her fatigue, but this has become our nightly ritual. Tea with Sidonie, and if we are lucky, some insight into the life of the woman accused of arson.

Before we can enter the garden, a place that still beckons people like the flames of April 10, Sidonie is making her way to us. Pleasantries are perfunctory. Madeleine offers a bite to eat; Sidonie thanks her for the bread and cheese and puts it in her pocket. There is clearly something on her mind. She takes my arm and propels me away from those gathered outside the Hôtel-Dieu.

"Monsieur." There is an urgency to her voice. A tremor. Perhaps it is fear. Madeleine places her arm on Sidonie's.

"We are told Angélique may be tortured. Surely that is not so."

I can feel Sidonie's apprehension. I can sense Madeleine's shock and horror. I forget not everyone works in a world where punishment is meted out daily and is often unbearably painful.

"We should sit." I lead the women to a small table set up in the outdoor courtyard. We find ourselves some tea. Tension wraps itself around our cups, climbs the legs of our chairs, and seeps into the ground beneath our feet.

"The Criminal Ordinance permits torture for serious crimes." I lift my hand to ward off the protests. "There are reasons for this. The torture can help extract a confession. This is important to get to the truth of a matter. There is also the issue of accomplices. Torture can help to draw out names that would otherwise die on an accused's lips."

Sidonie grows white. She grips the table. Madeleine gasps. "Surely not."

"Most certainly," I say. "It is not pleasant, for anyone. But it is necessary in the pursuit of justice."

I sip my tea and hope the women will follow suit. This will help to calm them. Quietly I point out. "We have another suspect in this case. If Angélique is found guilty, if she does not confess...

There is no need to say more. Tears are slowly making their way down Sidonie's cheeks. Madeleine is looking at me with an expression I have not seen before. I do not like it.

"Tell us about the torture."

Now I am shocked. "Mais non! Madeleine, this is too much. You are with child. Sidonie is ailing with the weight of the last few days. We must let this go."

The two women look directly at me. The look is the same on both faces: resolve.

* * *

Torment in New France is meted out in two steps. We have what we call la question ordinaire, which is not at all like it sounds. This is the first attempt at attaining an admission of guilt or the naming of a co-conspirator. It usually works. No one wants to go through this pain twice.

Few do. The second phase is called la question extraordinaire, which is much closer to what it sounds. The agony is greater, more pronounced.

I try to explain this process to the two women sitting beside me, mouths open, eyes wide, tea cold. I try to gloss over the implements of pain required to extract answers to questions ordinary and extraordinary: thumbscrews, racks, binding cloth.

"Surely not," says Madeleine.

Her horror is understandable, and I wonder why I have not questioned this judicial process until now. I wonder if it needs questioning, or if my agreeing to discuss torture with women is what really needs to be questioned.

"The brodequins." Sidonie's voice is barely above a whisper.

Now it is my turn to be shocked. How would a teenage servant girl know about this? Who has she been talking to? Or eavesdropping on?

I shake my head no. On this I am firm.

* * *

It is clear I would last mere seconds when faced with any device of torture. One look from my wife and I find myself explaining about the boot, a form of torture that is so painful recipients prefer death to remaining alive.

"There is a large chair. Here the accused sits. Planks are placed on either side of both legs and bound with rope. Wedges are driven between the planks."

"But that would tighten the planks even more!" Madeleine is looking at me like she does not know me. "Certainly, non, this could only happen once."

If you confess. If you don't, there will be three more strikes with the hammer. In phase two, there will be eight strikes.

Sidonie sits upright. She brings her shoulder blades together. The resolve is back. "If this is what must be done to get an honest confession, this is what must be done." She takes a sip of her cold tea. "Now we must move on to other things."

* * *

Madeleine does not move on as easily as Sidonie, but she leaves well enough alone. We finish our tea, such as it is, and our conversation, such as it is.

My wife is quiet on the walk home. I ask if she is all right.

"I am ashamed of my ignorance."

"What do you mean? You are the most intelligent woman I know."

"And yet I know nothing about our laws that allow torture or wood that has been shaped into planks for the sole purpose of pain."

"You do not need to know of these things," I assure her.

"We all need to know about these things."

Chapter 8
Testimony
Monday, April 19, 1734

April 19, 1734

Cher Maman, Papa,

It has been almost ten days since the fire. It seems like only yesterday, and it seems like a lifetime ago. It consumes life in Montréal. The lower town is still a shambles, but there is some order to that disarray now. Many people have found temporary accommodation to carry them through the rebuilding phase, which is slowly starting.

It is not only the material that has been affected. There is an energy here that is uncomfortable at best, harsh at its worst. The townspeople want Angélique to hang. They want her to pay for what they are convinced she did in the most definitive way imaginable. At least they want someone to pay, and for now, that someone is Angélique.

I do not believe I have told you about Sidonie. She is a servant who worked in the house next door to the de Francheville home.

She knows Angélique. It is hard to say whether she likes her or not, whether she admires her, pities her, or resents her. I suspect that mélange of emotions is common. I fear I have them all at times.

As special rapporteur, of course, I must keep my emotions in check. My role is to be objective. To report on the facts, to identify discrepancies, to highlight areas for further investigation. It is a job I must admit I am enjoying, although I worry if I am doing it justice.

I share with you another worry: Madeleine has joined me in my nighty meetings with Sidonie. We have tea in the Hôtel-Dieu. Some evenings, most evenings, this is enjoyable. I must remind myself this is not friends gathered for a pleasant interlude. And often the conversation focuses on unpleasant topics. Tonight, I am somewhat embarrassed to say, we talked about torture.

I think back to life in Acadie. We discussed many things – land, children, weddings and funerals, weather (always the weather), the neighbours' behaviour even. Yet we never talked about torment and agony. Somehow this has become part of that fabric that weaves throughout daily life in Montréal. It is a thread we did not pull until recently. Now we yank it out and lay it under the brilliance of the sun for all to see.

There are many times I wish to cover my eyes.

Your loving son,
Philippe

PS We speak only of fluffy clouds and warm, sunny days to the little one. And of course, we tell him (I believe) often about his grand-mère and grand-père.

Chapter 9
Testimony
Saturday, May 1, 1734

The past two weeks have been quiet. Refreshingly so. Regretfully so. We continue to have tea with Sidonie, but we talk less about the fire and its after-effects and more about our daily lives in Montréal. These are short conversations, but they seem to be important to Sidonie, and I know they are important to me. I feel less like I have used the servant solely for information and more like she has become another person I know in this town and enjoy spending time with. Madeleine also feels it is important to maintain contact with Sidonie. Perhaps we hold out the illusion of family.

There has been no sign of Claude Thibault. Literally. It is like the man has dropped off the map of New France. I suspect by now he has. Two weeks is plenty of time to get to New England and from there to France. Or perhaps *La Louisiane.* But if Thibault does not like Montréal, he is unlikely to care for life in another French colony.

Henri Geôlier disagrees with my theory. He believes Thibault is still close at hand, waiting for the furor over the fire and the trial to die down. That could be a while. "The man can wait this out," the jailer contends. "What else does he have to do?"

"But someone would have to hide him. Who would be so foolish?" This is a point I make almost every lunch we share (although "share" mistakenly implies an equal division of food).

Today Monsieur Geôlier answers my question. Between a mouthful of egg and cheese he informs me that the slave has still refused to admit Claude Thibault helped her set the lower town ablaze. "She says she did not start the fire. She says her lover did not start the fire."

"Why protect the man if he is guilty?" I am talking more to myself, but Monsieur Geôlier responds.

"She is a woman. She is in lo-o-o-ve." He draws the last word out with derision.

"She may well be, but I'm not sure the bonds of love are stronger than the stench and vermin of a prison cell. I'm sure you have seen strong men give up under these conditions."

Monsieur Geôlier looks at me with some surprise. I am assuming my point has hit home. I am wrong. "Aah, mon ami. You have not met the soldier Thibault, the fur trader, the man of the world."

I'm not sure what that has to do with anything. Monsieur Geôlier assures me it is at the heart of why an imprisoned slave would not denounce her lover and the reason why someone – and by someone we mean a woman – would squirrel away a man in the midst of a manhunt.

"Are you saying Thibault had other lovers?"

The derision is back. "To hear him tell it, he had many other lovers. They swooned at his feet."

"Do you believe him?"

"Do I believe women would like a little comfort, a little warmth, a warm caress."

Point taken. "But surely that would make Angélique more likely to give up her lover now. To name him as the person who set the fire."

Monsieur Geôlier shakes his head. "It is sad how little you know about women."

* * *

I do know the law and the legal landscape. This is familiar territory, and we are back to where we were two weeks ago: testimony. Judge Raimbault is leaving no stone unturned. I am reassured by his persistence at getting to the truth of what happened on April 10.

The first witness of the day and thirteenth of the trial is Louis Langlois dit Traversy, a tenant farmer who lives on the de Francheville homestead in Coste St. Michel. He says that eight or nine days after Angélique was returned to her mistress following her attempted escape, he was in the de Francheville kitchen in Montréal. Angélique was also there.

He told her she was evil, that she should not have fled as she did, and that if Madame de Francheville had wished, Angélique would be in prison. He warned Angélique her mistress might sell her. It was Angélique's reply, as told by the farm labourer, that was both expected and shocking. "That damned whore, if she sells me, she will sorely regret it." Monsieur Traversy asked her "What will you do?"

Here's what Angélique said, "We do not state our intentions; the snow will melt away, the earth will show itself anew and tracks will not be left behind."

The meaning was clear to anyone who had read Angélique's arrest report: she was planning to run away again. This time she'd leave no tracks in the snow to reveal her whereabouts.

Monsieur Traversy's wife was the second and final witness of the day. Marie-Françoise Thomelet says she pressed Angélique "to be a good Christian and act well." She warned the slave if she did not appease her mistress, she would be sold, to which the slave responded, "She would sorely repent, I would have her burned."

Madame Thomelet warned Angélique if she carried through on her threats, she would be hanged, she would die. Angélique said this was of no concern to her.

I wonder if she still feels the same way.

* * *

Judge Raimbault has inspired me. I watch him interview the witnesses. There is a professional distance yet a forging of common ground. It is as if he says to them without saying anything, "I understand what you are feeling. I know this is a strange environment, a sad time. We will get through this. Justice will be served."

This will not be the tone he takes with Angélique, of course, but for these men and women it is appropriate, and it is effective. We learn more than we did before they testified. Yet, and I would not say this to Judge Raimbault, we have not the irrefutable evidence to answer the question "Who started the fire?"

We are running out of time. The trial cannot go on much longer. Not everyone remotely connected to Angélique can be called to testify. The evidence we need may not lie with the men, women, and children connected to the fire on rue Saint-Paul. It may lie with the slave who lies several feet from us in a cell unable to hear the evidence against her.

She will. Not today, but soon.

In the meantime, Judge Raimbault continues onward. It is that commitment, in particular, that has inspired me. I wonder if perhaps I have been too easily dissuaded, too polite.

I discuss this with Madeleine over dinner. I describe Judge Raimbault and his approach, his confidence, and the message he sends gently but firmly to all who come before him: Do not try to fool me.

"Do you think people try to fool you?" My wife asks this in an even tone. I sense no judgment, but I do sense something I can't quite put my finger on.

"I think we all have secrets. We all have things we are reluctant to discuss."

"You would like to draw those secrets out."

"Only if they are relevant to the case at hand."

"And who decides that?"

"Ultimately, Judge Raimbault and the tribunal, the notaries, but it is my job to gather as much background information as I can. This will add perspective and nuance to the deliberations."

"So, speaking of things we are reluctant to discuss," my wife says, "what is really bothering you?"

I mull this question over in my mind as we make our way to what remains of the Hôtel-Dieu. Madeleine invariably sees what I cannot, perhaps because of reluctance or blindness or naivety. If being special rapporteur has taught me one thing it is this: There is much about daily life in Montréal that I did just not know, I never imagined.

* * *

Sidonie has tea ready on a small table. It is a mild night, the sun stays with us longer now, and I find myself looking forward to the evening. I remind myself that is not why I am here. That is not what Judge Raimbault would be thinking.

Sidonie looks much better than she did the first few days after the fire. Her colour is back. She seems less weary. There are no pain lines etched in her face. I tell her she looks healthy. She seems to like the compliment.

"We are all moving on, finding our footing now. The fire was a very bad time for us all. It took a toll."

"They cannot find Claude Thibault."

Madeleine sits back and looks at me askance. Sidonie spills some of her tea. I feel badly about my abrupt change of subject, but I am rather pleased at my approach. I think Judge Raimbault would approve.

"Did you think they would?" Madeleine asks. Now it is my turn to look surprised. Sidonie continues to wipe up her tea.

"Did you not?"

"No. He is long gone. That is the smart thing to do. He is a smart man would you say." Madeleine turns to Sidonie. "You knew him." We have flustered her. This is not our usual tone over tea.

Sidonie ponders the question. "He is certainly not a stupid man. But more than smart, I would say he is a man with a mission. He loathes Montréal. He wants to leave here, and he will find a way to freedom outside New France."

That makes sense. What does not make sense is the feeling of pride I hear in Sidonie's voice. I wonder if this young servant girl would also like to find freedom outside New France. "The jailer disagrees."

Now I have everyone's attention. "Monsieur Geôlier believes Thibault is right here in Montréal or close by. He believes someone is hiding him."

"Why would someone do that?" Madeleine asks. "It is not smart. It is not the path a man on a mission would take."

"Perhaps it is smart," I counter. "The police cannot go door to door to find this man. But they can follow the roadways. They can ask travellers. They can search the woods. All the time, peut-être, he is right here safe in someone's attic or basement."

I look at Sidonie. She has gone pale. "What do you think?"

"I think your wife is right, Monsieur. Montréal is not safe surely and Thibault would run toward safety, not away from it."

We all pause for a moment. I reflect on the conversation and wonder at its usefulness. The two women sip their tea.

"Who would hide him?" It is, of course, the critical question, and it is, of course, my wife who brings us to the heart of the matter.

Sidonie jumps in. "That is right. They have already interviewed everyone even remotely close to him."

This is true, but it may not be the whole truth. "Monsieur Geôlier posits there is another woman. Perhaps more than one."

It is my night to shock the two women who are helping me succeed as special rapporteur. For this, I feel a sense of shame. Then I think of Judge Raimbault.

"Surely not," says Madeleine. I hear the shock and disapproval in her voice. I place my hand over hers. This is the wrong move, but I am not sure why.

"That is jailhouse gossip," Sidonie says and dismisses the idea with a wave of her hand.

"It is more than that." I have, once again, the undivided attention of the two women. I am not sure I like being caught in their gaze. "Thibault told the jailer he had many women, not just Angélique. He made it sound like he was a renowned coureur de jupons. A philanderer."

"You think one of these many women is hiding him." As only Madeleine can do, she asks a question and makes a statement simultaneously.

"I think it is possible. I think it might also explain why the police have been unsuccessful in the search."

"You knew him," Madeleine says, turning to Sidonie. "What do you think?"

"I know longer know what to think, Madame."

Chapter 10
Testimony
Sunday, May 2, 1734

Rolant is not impressed with the jailer's theory on the whereabouts of Claude Thibault. "He is long gone, I fear. We must accept that fact and move on."

"You believe the police would have caught him by now if he were still in Montréal?"

"I believe Thibault is far too savvy to hang around a town or a colony when there is a military ordinance for his arrest. He will get away from New France as quickly as is humanly possible."

"That will put a burden on the court to prove his complicity in the fire."

"It is unlikely he would confess even if captured. Our best chance at proving his guilt is if Angélique admits he was involved. In all likelihood he was the mastermind."

This assumption is a tenet of French law. Women are presumed not to have the wherewithal to instigate a crime. That is a man's work. Women follow. I am not sure, however, that the lawmakers ever met anyone like Angélique. Who may not be guilty, I remind myself. The same could be said for Thibault.

I realize my discussions with Sidonie have focused on where the former soldier may be hiding, not why the former soldier would set Madame de Francheville's house on fire. I will follow this line of inquiry tonight.

As it turns out, the line of inquiry will be pursued much earlier.

* * *

My superior continues to support my work as special rapporteur, but I sense the wheels of justice are turning more insistently toward a verdict of guilty for Angélique. This may well be the fair and just verdict, but Rolant, on orders from at least some members of the tribunal, is to leave no stone unturned. I am the stone turner.

Lunch is bread, smoked ham, and fruit. And Henri Geôlier. The jailer is particularly effusive today. He regales me with tales of those who have made their way into his cells, and in some cases, their way out. This is interesting but not why I share my food with a man I'm not sure even likes me.

The jailer does get points for astuteness though. "Aah, I bore you."

"Not at all. The prison holds many fascinating tales."

"What tale would you like me to tell?"

"I seek your advice." Monsieur Geôlier seems as taken aback by this statement as I am. I feel the need to explain. "In my role as special rapporteur ...."

I get no further. The big man's hand comes down on the desk, he leans back. He laughs, and he laughs. He laughs so hard tears stream down his face. His belly shakes from the exertion. He looks at me. And he laughs some more. I do not get the joke.

My confusion must be obvious. "Tell me Monsieur Archambeau, what are the responsibilities of the special rapporteur." There is a derogatory inflection on the last two words that I choose to ignore. I explain my role with pride.

"Aah, the burden." The inflection is back. "Tell me Monsieur Archambeau, when the court appointed you special rapporteur, did they give you more money, perhaps a junior clerk to work with you, an office?"

Point made. I have a title without the trimmings. "It is like the stores along the lower town, the wall marts, they have the most wonderful designations for their people. But there is little recompense."

"It does not diminish the work they do," I point out.

The jailer gives me credit for this observation. "You are right, Monsieur. How can I help?"

The straightforward question and the sincerity with which it was delivered sets me back. Perhaps I have been too harsh in my judgment of Monsieur Geôlier. "We debate whether Claude Thibault would flee town or stay put. The real question though is why would he start a fire at Madame de Francheville's house?"

Monsieur Geôlier looks at me carefully. I do not know how to read the look, but I know I should. There is something here. Then the moment passes. "There are many reasons why the man would commit arson. I am sure you know this. He wanted money from the de Franchevilles. He wanted his own freedom from indenture. He wanted out of New France without any incumbrances."

These are all valid reasons, and yet they do not seem enough somehow. It is like the jailer can read my mind. "You do not think these are sufficient." It is a statement, and it is accurate. What is unclear: why do I feel this way?

"I would trust your judgment, Philippe. It is sound." I do not know what startles me more, the jailer's support or the use of my first name.

* * *

Busy work keeps me at my desk for the remainder of the afternoon. It is work that needs to be done and will help in the final analysis of Angélique's guilt, but it is not work that requires my full attention. I play my conversation with Monsieur Geôlier over and over in my mind. As I prepare to put away my work for the day, I am no further ahead. Supper with Madeleine and a walk to the merchants' quarter will give me a much-needed reprieve.

As I am clearing my desk, Rolant arrives. There is an energy here I have not felt before. I look up with some concern.

"Angélique will be interrogated tomorrow afternoon."

The papers I am holding fall to the floor. This is not a surprise. It is what happens next in a trial, and yet it seems too soon. I have so much more work to do.

* * *

It is all anyone can talk about. We hear the chatter as we make our way to the lower town.

"She will appear tomorrow."

"She must tell the truth. She must sign an oath."

"She will confess. Everyone confesses."

"She is guilty. She has destroyed our home."

The conversation cannot be ignored, and yet, listening seems intrusive. "Do you think Angélique is guilty?" Madeleine turns from those around us. This is a question she has not asked before. I want to give it the weight it deserves.

"I don't know. But I trust the court. I trust the process."

My wife looks away from me. "You are too trusting."

***

Sidonie is waiting for us, and there is no pretence of a casual running into one another. "Have you heard?"

"I think they have heard back in France," I say. "It is all anyone is talking about."

"What does it mean?" Sidonie asks.

I am not sure how to interpret the question. What does it mean for Angélique? For the trial? For the march toward justice?

"It is part of the process." I am avoiding the bigger discussion inherent in Sidonie's question. I know it. She knows it. My wife knows it. Sidonie may be willing to accept that answer; Madeleine is not.

"Will they hand down a verdict tomorrow?"

"If she confesses."

"Angélique will never confess," says Sidonie firmly.

"Interrogation is difficult," I say. Two faces look at me. They want more. "Questions will be fired at Angélique. She will be expected to answer quickly. Speed is associated with honesty."

"Why?" my wife asks. It is a question I have never asked myself. I take a moment to reflect.

"See," Madeleine says before I can speak. "You reflect on questions of importance. You take time with your answer. To make sure it is correct, complete."

"That is true," I concede, "but it implies the question is one you did not anticipate. Angélique will be asked questions she should know the answer to right away. There will be no need for hesitation."

"What happens after the questions? When is this over?" Sidonie sounds distraught, and I am reminded that this servant girl knew Angélique, had conversations with her in the street, looked at the stars with her, complained, I am sure, about their mistresses.

"If Angélique confesses, the trial will end. If she contends she is innocent, the court may recall witnesses to confirm their testimony. Then there is the confrontation."

I refuse to look at either woman, but I feel their gaze on me. My chest tightens. "Angélique and her accusers will meet. She can confront them, refute what they have to say, perhaps explain a misunderstanding."

"There is no misunderstanding here," Sidonie says.

"You think Angélique is guilty," I say. I am surprised.

"It does not matter," says Sidonie. "She will burn."

* * *

Timeline. It has occurred to me that I should review the timeline of the fire with

Sidonie. I am embarrassed to admit, it will also distract us from the topic at hand. I explain the importance of understanding precisely what happened when, and why the judge and prosecutor dwell on this theme.

"There can be no contradictions."

Two blank faces look at me. "It would help me Sidonie, if you could tell me where you were and what was going on when you first realized there was a fire."

"I have told you this. I was on the main floor. In the living room. I was cleaning up. I looked out the window. Kids were playing outside. Everything was normal.

"Then it was not."

Madeleine pats Sidonie's hand. I feel bad for making her relive that horrific night, but somehow, I feel this is important. I feel the pressure of the trial as it moves closer and closer to a resolution.

"Someone outside yells 'Fire.' I am not sure who. Angélique perhaps, or Marie-Manon. I run outside. We all hug each other as the flames consume the street."

There is more hand patting on Madeleine's part, more head hanging on mine. "I did not expect that."

"Expect what?"

Sidonie looks at me in some surprise. She has been talking to herself. "The fury of the fire. I thought the house would burn. It never occurred to me all the houses would burn."

That realization is not unique to Sidonie. I remember as we passed water bucket after water bucket thinking that surely we would quench these flames. We did not.

* * *

Something is nagging at me on the walk home. Madeleine asks what is bothering. I focus on the question. The answer: Sidonie's complete assurance in the outcome of a trial that is still under way and has been diligently pursuing the truth for more than three weeks. "I am surprised at such a belief."

"You are surprised at the lack of faith in your beloved justice system."

"Are you not?" I ask. "Without such faith, there is no justice."

"Do you think Angélique will get justice?"

Chapter 11
Interrogation
Monday, May 3, 1734

A small handful of men command the room. They are holding court, literally, in the town jail. Their authority is unquestioned. Their presence the ultimate symbol of justice. I feel small. I feel proud.

Interrogation is a cornerstone of a criminal trial where the punishment is potentially death. The accused sits on the criminal seat, a low wooden bench. She must look up at these men.

Preliminaries dispensed, Judge Raimbault dives in. There is no gentle lead up to tougher questions, no exchange of pleasantries or tossing out of obvious questions.

"Why did you and Claude Thibault set fire to Madame de Francheville's house?"

Angélique looks unperturbed. "I never spoke of this to Thibault nor to anyone else, nor did I have the urge to commit such a deed."

Judge Raimbault persists – and reveals what may well be his view of what happened on April 10. "Is it not true that Thibault in retaliation for being put in prison urged you to set fire to the attic of Madame de Francheville's home?"

"No." It is a simple answer. It is fast. I am not sure if it is truthful.

The judge ignores the denial. "Tell us what time you made your way to the attic carrying embers. Tell us where the fire started."

Angélique sticks to her story. "I took no embers to the attic. The only time I was in the attic that day was in the morning and my mistress was with me. I do not know where the fire began."

"Yet you were taken aback when you went up to the attic with Sieur Radisson."

"I was taken aback at seeing the fire in the attic. There was not even a fire lit in the chimneys of the house."

"Why did you tell Sieur Radisson there was no ladder when he asked for one to throw water on the flames?"

"We did not talk about a ladder for this purpose. There was a staircase and ladders to reach the pigeon nests. He wanted a ladder because that stairway was no longer usable, and he wanted to salvage what he could."

Judge Raimbault tries again to trip up Angélique. He asks if she went to the attic the evening of the fire, at 5 p.m. The slave reiterates that she did not go to the attic that day except in the morning. A line has been drawn. I wonder if Angélique will cross it.

This thread of questioning has ended. Judge Raimbault moves on. He asks about statements she made to Marie-Manon. "Did you not say, 'That bitch there will not laugh so much later, as she will not sleep in her house'?"

Angélique denies ever having said that to the Panis slave or to anyone.

Judge Raimbault makes another abrupt shift. "Did Thibault tell you your mistress had sold you?"

Another denial, but this one is qualified. "From time to time, I was told, even by the valet of Monsieur le Commissaire, that I was to be sent to the islands because I ran away with Thibault. Ten to twelve days prior to the fire, Madame de Francheville told me that she had written to the intendant to sell me, that I was too malicious, and she no longer wanted me in her service, that she was always in a confrontation with me, her servant, that she did not like at all to hear noise in her house and that this was always the case. I told Madame I did not want to be dismissed from her service. I said she could send away her other servant; I would fare well on my own, and Madame would be pleased with me. This is why Madame de Francheville told the servant to go and hire herself out by the month. She could return when I was no longer in her service."

I am rapidly making notes. In cases where I want to return to a statement for further reflection or investigation, I make a mark in the margin. This is one of those cases. I am impressed and, truth be told, surprised at the consistency of Angélique's answers, from the initial interrogation and during this current barrage of questions.

Written reports make the process sound moderated, even respectful. It is anything but. Pierre Raimbault is a seasoned inquisitor. He is clever, and he is persistent. His entire demeanor speaks to his confidence in getting to the truth and brooking no quarter. If I were Angélique, I would be frightened. Yet she holds herself with dignity. She holds her own. I will tell Madeleine this. It will give her some comfort.

* * *

There is little time to silently commend Judge Raimbault or the slave who holds her head high. The interrogation continues without a moment for breath or reflection. A series of questions are fired at Angélique. It is unclear if they are diversionary or if this is a trap into which the guilty might stumble.

"Did your mistress not chastise you on the day of the fire? Did you not head to the kitchen and sulk?"

"No. She was hardly in the house on that day."

"Before the fire started, did you not seek out the Panis girl, your neighbour, and tickle her being told she was in no humour to laugh? Did you not return to your mistress's house but reappear quickly with the Panis slave and say, 'Lady de Francheville is laughing heartily, but she will not be in her house for long. She will not sleep there'?"

"I wished to laugh with Marie-Manon."

"Did you not tell Marguerite de Couagne and Charlotte Desrivières to come inside the house?"

"I wanted them to enter the house. They were playing in the street where there was mud; little de Couagne had only shoes on her feet."

"Why on three or four occasions when you were in the street, did you look toward the roof of your mistress's house?"

"I went numerous times into the street. I did not look at all toward the roof of the house, having no reason to do so."

Angélique's replies are, to my untrained ear, prompt. In a French court, this is indicative of truthfulness. She does not delay, nor does she call into question the statements of others. She merely says what she did or did not do, and in some cases why. I wonder how Judge Raimbault is interpreting these responses. If he sees a wiliness I do not.

As if tuned to my internal dialogue, the judge pursues a new line of questioning. Perhaps, he poses, it was the harshness and reproach of Madame de Francheville that compelled Angélique to menace her mistress, to threaten to see her burned or to slash her throat. Angélique does not rise to the bait. She states, again, she never menaced Madame de Francheville. I make a mark in the margin. Surely, this is not true. There is enough evidence, and much of it direct, to refute this claim.

Judge Raimbault continues down this path undeterred. He never lets on whether he feels the court is making headway or Angélique has misstepped. Now he repeats previous testimony contending she would have any Frenchmen perish and burned like dogs if she were ever back in her home country. Angélique doesn't miss a beat. In fact, she turns the tables, somewhat, on her mistress. The slave says sometimes Madame de Francheville mistreated her, not often, but when she did Angélique would get angry and leave the house, but she never said anything like the court just stated.

Interestingly, Judge Raimbault asks when Madame de Francheville last mistreated Angélique. I do not know if this is a deliberate attempt to placate the accused or whether he believes her. The answer: Not since the death of her husband. I make a note in the margin. That was six months ago.

Now, there is a direct accusation.

> *"Is it not true that you intended when you took the embers up to the attic to cause the whole of the said house to be set ablaze, as well as others."*
>
> "I did not set the fire."

Judge Raimbault leaves this thread behind. I wonder if he got what he needed, and what he expected. He takes Angélique and those of us in the courtroom to the night of the fire. He asks about the two men who were with Angélique drinking syrup in the garden of the Hôtel-Dieu. He asks about the green blanket. The slave says she left the two men and went to lie down on some straw bedding near a doorway. The green blanket came from the hospital. She used it to wrap around her dirty skirts. She also denied having a falling out with Madame de

Francheville's servant or drinking brandy except when it was proffered by an assistant some mornings, as it was to the servant.

I am, admittedly, confused by this line of questioning. Judge Raimbault does not waste words or time. There is purpose to his inquiries, if only to ensure every opportunity is given to Angélique to respond to accusations or mire herself in them.

It is time to introduce Claude Thibault into evidence.

"Did you not steal three deerskins and numerous other items when you fled with Thibault?"

"I did not steal anything. Nor did Thibault."

"Some days prior to the fire, did you not see and speak on many occasions to Thibault, even on the night and the day following the fire, and on the day that you were sent to gaol."

"I spoke to him but on two occasions prior to the fire, when he went to settle his account with Madame de Francheville and on the day of the fire when he helped to salvage. He left before I was arrested."

More denials follow in rapid-fire succession. Angélique says she never told the widow Geoffrion she would not be at the de Francheville house for long. She denies telling the tenant farmer her mistress would regret it if she sold her. There is no vehemence here, no outrage. This speaks well for the slave, I think. Or is this an accomplished liar?

We are at the end of the interrogation. Angélique's testimony is read aloud. She is unable to sign. She does not know how. But she attests the answers are accurate and honest.

I do not know whether to believe her.

* * *

Madeleine wants details. She's dying to know not just what was said but how it was said. How did I react to what was said? Ultimately, do I believe Angélique?

Kindness precludes my wife from asking these questions as soon as I walk in the door, or over a meal of hot stew, or even as we make our way to the lower town. There is no need for me to tell the story twice, or for her to hear it repeated.

Sidonie does not have my wife's patience. She grabs my arm and leads me to a small table as soon as she sees us on the street. I retell the events of the afternoon. It takes almost as long as the interrogation itself.

There are two gasps. Madeleine inhales sharply when told Angélique denied ever menacing her mistress. The second sharp intake of breath comes from Sidonie when Angélique says Claude Thibault had no involvement in starting the fire.

135

It is a good tale, and I tell it well. I understand the judicial process and can explain what happened and why. I am also a good observer and add colourful comments as appropriate. In the end though, both women want to know the same thing. *What does it mean?*

There is little I can say. There is no answer to the question. Angélique has drawn her line in the sand. She has made her statements and attested to their veracity. There is no backing down from this now. The real question is whether the court believes her, particularly Judge Raimbault.

I have no idea.

* * *

Sidonie says she has asked around, quietly, about Claude Thibault and received the same answer. No one has seen him. "Everyone thinks he is long gone."

I will not say the police have given up. I do not know this to be true, and even if it were, there is no benefit in announcing that to nearby ears. However, it is most likely they have moved on to other matters and left Claude Thibault to fend for himself wherever he may be.

"What if they can't find him?" Madeleine asks.

"He will be a hunted man."

Two more gasps. "Surely, you can expect nothing less," I say. "There is a warrant for his arrest. He has not turned himself in to the authorities."

"Neither is he guilty," says my wife.

"Neither has he been found guilty." I correct my wife gently. She rewards me with a look that is anything but gentle.

"Why won't the court leave him alone?" My wife nods her approval at Sidonie's question.

"He is a suspect in arson, perhaps the most significant arson in the history of New France. The court has a duty to determine his role. Judge Raimbault will take that duty seriously."

"What can the court do to him?" Sidonie asks.

This is a gasp-worthy question and one I was hoping to avoid. "That will depend on whether he is deemed to have been involved in the crime."

"How can they ever know that?" Madeleine asks. She deduces the answer before I can speak. I see the distress in her face.

"I do not understand," says Sidonie.

"If Angélique says Thibault was involved, he will be deemed to be guilty," I explain softly.

"Why would Angélique ever do that?" Sidonie asks. She, too, answers her own question. "Mon Dieu. The brodequins."

* * *

It is a quiet walk home. Not the comfortable kind of serenity where Madeleine nestles into my shoulder, and we make our way slowly and contentedly. The other kind of quiet. The kind where we are holding hands, and it feels like there is a whole world dividing us.

Finally, my wife speaks. "I do not think I like Montréal. It feels less like home every day."

Until tonight, these words would have been music to my ears. They might be the opening I needed to discuss Acadie and the possibility of living in another part of New France. A part where people farmed and fished, where they did not live behind walls for fear of the British. They moved in the open. They celebrated life. Tonight is not the time for this conversation despite the overture my wife has given me. Hers is a statement tinged with disappointment and shame. I do not want my home tainted with this hue.

As Madeleine climbs under the bedcovers, she asks, "When will this be over?"

I fear for my wife this may never be over. I fear for Angélique this may be over far too soon.

***

May 3, 1734

Cher Maman, Papa,

I write with a heart full of joy and a heavy heart. Madeleine and the little one are doing well. My wife is round and healthy. She smiles when she touches her belly. We laugh when the baby kicks. The baby kicks a lot. I believe it is a boy.

Montréal is struggling, however. The fire has left more than ash and soot in its wake. Families have scattered throughout the town and beyond searching for accommodation. Friends and family have reached out to help, and the sisters of the Hôtel-Dieu are doing all they can to assist the ill and the homeless as is their mission: to care for the sick and impoverished, men, women, Indigenous, and French alike.

As I write this, I am reminded that the sisters, too, are homeless, and not for the first time. This is the third fire to raze the hospital. In the winter of 1695, the building was completely destroyed. Miraculously, a new and larger hospital was rebuilt before the new year arrived. Two and a half decades later, another firestorm. Another loss of the entire Hôtel-Dieu. This time it took three years before the hospital was fully reconstructed. I fear this time it will take even longer. It may well take a decade.

This is the physical environment that surrounds us at the moment: destruction, debris, desolation. Then there is the trial. Fourteen witnesses have testified. To date.

Judge Raimbault is determined to leave no stone unturned, no voice unheard. You would like him.

The slave, Marie-Joseph Angélique, was confronted by the court this week. It is all the town can talk about. It weighs on Madeleine, and on me. The slave was consistent in her answers to the court. I did not start the fire. I did not threaten my mistress.

I would like to believe her. I do not know that I do, but something gnaws at my stomach. Despite the testimony of so many people, much of what we have is hearsay. Much of what I have documented as special rapporteur is second hand. The fact is no one saw who started the fire, at least no one is coming forward to irrefutably point the finger of blame.

Maman, Papa, I apologize for this letter. I sound ungrateful. I am not. I love my job, and I believe very firmly in the court and the work it does. I know I am fortunate to be here, and I thank Uncle Jean every day for reaching across the ocean from Versailles to get me fulfilling employment in Montréal. I have you both to thank for supporting me in this endeavour.

Still, I think often of Acadie. I miss the sun dancing on the Baie Française. I miss the strength of the dykes, the smell of fresh earth, the growth of barley, rye, corn. I miss you.

Your loving son,
Philippe

PS You must send us your favorite baby names. We are getting close!

Chapter 12
Interrogation
Tuesday, May 4, 1734

Something is afoot. There is a flurry of activity at the courthouse. People scurry to and fro, but I wonder if they are really going anywhere. Judge Raimbault and Sieur Foucher are locked behind closed doors. There are matters of import being discussed while others scuttle throughout the building.

I sit at my desk and work to remain calm. My role is to document, to investigate. I am doing that. If there is more I am to do, or more I am to know, Rolant will tell me.

Turns out it is not Rolant who tells me what is happening all around me.

Henri Geôlier arrives for lunch on time and on cue. "Cold stew. My favourite."

I suspect Madeleine knows this. That lunch is more about what would please the jailer than her husband. Today, the gift of food is reciprocated with an offering up of information.

"You feel the energy, eh?"

"It is hard to miss the activity."

"Aah, but you do not know its cause. I thought you would."

There is nothing I can say to this. To defend my lack of knowledge would be silly, to pretend indifference would be sillier.

"You do, I presume."

The jailer nods between mouthfuls of stew and bread. "The trial is not over."

This I knew. "We are waiting for a verdict."

"You will wait some time."

I give Monsieur Geôlier points for knowing how to tell a story. How to build the drama and keep the listener hanging on. "What do you mean?"

"There will be more witnesses."

"Surely not! There have been fourteen already. For three weeks, we have heard testimony. There have been two interrogations of the slave."

"There will be more."

I do not know if this brevity is the jailer's storytelling finesse or an inability to say more with his mouth full. I wait. He chews.

At last, Monsieur Geôlier puts his bowl down. He leans in. I follow suit. "I am told there may be another ten witnesses called. The trial may last another three weeks."

I sit back in surprise. "This is unbelievable." I do not doubt the veracity of the jailer's pronouncement or the accuracy of his sources. But a trial of this length and magnitude is virtually unheard of. The resources, time, and effort required will be substantial. Part of me is proud of the French justice system, a system that would invest such resources in determining the truth. I credit Judge Raimbault.

Another part of me, a part buried much deeper, wonders if we need to demonstrate no stone has been left unturned before we condemn a woman to death based primarily on rumour and innuendo.

* * *

As usual, the jailer's information proves beyond reproof. Rolant stops by after lunch. He takes one look at my face. "So, you have heard."

"I have heard the trial will continue. There are more witnesses."

"There may be many more witnesses."

"Where are they coming from?"

"There is no doubt Judge Raimbault is thorough, but your reports are also playing a role here. You have provided timelines and details that have helped identify other witnesses. The court is pleased."

As am I. This is high praise, and it confirms the importance of the special rapporteur's job. Still ....

"You are not satisfied."

I rush to reassure my superior I am delighted to know my work has been helpful, proud that the court seeks to ensure justice is done. "I wonder though what more there is to learn. Definitive proof seems elusive if not impossible."

"We shall let the court do its work. You may be surprised at what more there is to discover."

* * *

Madeleine is pleased to hear the court is not rushing to judgment. "We will all feel better knowing that every effort was made to learn exactly what happened on April 10 and precisely who is to blame. I am reassured."

This is the opening I have been waiting for. "I am glad you feel better. That makes me happy. Have you, perhaps, changed your mind about Montréal?"

My wife knows whereof I speak. She knows I harbour a desire to return to my home, to Acadie, to gardens with peas and carrots, to oats and barley waving in the wind, to family. "I think this is a discussion for another time. But that time is coming quickly."

I love this woman.

* * *

Sidonie does not seem to share my wife's enthusiasm for an extended trial. I do not know if this is simply surprise at the news or if she shares my unspoken fear. "Why, why would they do this?"

"I do not know," I answer truthfully, "but gathering more evidence can only help to bolster our understanding of what happened and who made it happen."

"You are worried about Angélique." Madeleine pats Sidonie's hand. The young girl is too upset to be comforted.

"I am worried about all of us. About this dragging on. We cannot move on with our lives. I do not understand why we all have to suffer."

"Closure will be all the more solid if it is built on a foundation of fact." I sound like an officious court clerk. I remind myself I am an officious court clerk.

Sidonie rises. There is anger in the straightening of her skirt, the movement of her chair. "The facts are these. There was a fire. There is a Black slave no one likes. She is nasty. She will burn."

* * *

The servant's vehemence has upset Madeleine. I share the confusion that lies at the heart of her distress. My wife is kinder.

"We have forgotten that this is Sidonie's life. She is not sitting on the sidelines observing the trial as if it were a lacrosse game. What happens has real consequences for her."

"Surely though there must be relief to know that Angélique is getting a fair trial. The verdict is not predetermined."

My wife sidesteps the implied question. "I will make pie for tomorrow. It will help Sidonie feel better."

For some reason, I feel worse.

Chapter 13
Interrogation
Wednesday, May 5, 1734

More witnesses will be heard tomorrow. Rolant has spent much of the morning at my desk. We are reviewing the witness list to see how we can help. First up will be Alexis Lemoine Monière.

I check my notes. He is Madame de Francheville's brother-in-law. Angélique stayed with him for a brief period. I did not speak with him directly.

"What do you think he will have to add?"

"I would guess Angélique did something when she stayed with him that will cast aspersions on her character."

My superior is right. Otherwise, why bring this man forward. Madame de Francheville has lots of relatives. "The second fire."

Rolant looks at me. There is slight amazement at the statement but also acceptance. He waits for me to work out my thinking in my mind. "There were earlier reports that the fire on rue Saint-Paul was not the first fire Angélique was accused of setting. I could find no one to verify this.

Perhaps it happened at Sieur Monière's house."

My superior nods, agreement and approval. "That would also help explain the presence of two other witnesses. Catherine Custeau is a servant of Sieur Monière's. So is Jacques Jalleteau."

An additional two witnesses are also slated to testify tomorrow: Ignace Gamelin and Jeanne Nafrechoux de Béréy. The former is a friend of Madame de Francheville and has done business with her and her husband. The latter, of course, lived next door to the de Franchevilles.

I have no idea why either are being called to attest. I wonder what I've missed.

Chapter 14
Interrogation
Thursday, May 6, 1734

It is as Rolant and I had suspected. Alexis Monière, the first witness deposed, says Angélique started a fire in his home long before the lower town burned.

He testifies that one or two days before Angélique ran away with Claude Thibault she was staying at his house because Madame de Francheville told him, "She didn't dare keep her in her home because she was malicious." During the night, the fifty-two-year-old merchant awoke to the smell of smoke. He searched the house but could not find any fire. The following day one of the servants reported to him that the fire had been started in the straw bedding or blanket used by Angélique "who had placed an extraordinary number of pieces of wood on and around the stove against which she was sleeping in the room."

One of the wood pieces made a noise that startled Angélique, Monsieur Monière was told, and she turned the straw bedding upside down to smother the fire. Interestingly, that same night Claude Thibault was sleeping with the other male servants in the storeroom below the kitchen, and his blanket caught fire. The next day he and Angélique escaped.

Two servants support Monsieur Monière's testimony. Catherine Custeau says Angélique and Claude Thibault went to bed early, but she worked late into the night having numerous chores to attend to. When she finally went to bed, she had to go past Angélique who was sleeping by the stove. Mademoiselle Custeau saw the bed on fire and poured a jug of water on it. Angélique told the servant to say nothing about the incident. Less than an hour later, Sieur Monière was awakened by smoke and began searching the entire house.

According to the twenty-five-year-old servant, she did not say anything to Sieur Moniere about what happened. She did not want him to be angry with Angélique. Her silence, however, did not extend to other members of the household. The next morning she told the other servants they risked being burned. In return, other domestic staff who had slept with Thibault said a fire had also started in their room. In fact, one of the men had his jacket, vest, and blanket burned as a result.

That man would be Jacques Jalleteau, the eighteenth witness to testify. The servant starts where so many earlier witnesses also began: declaring he has no knowledge of how the fire on April 10 originated. He did know, however, that the fire in Monsieur

Monière's house started in Angélique's blanket. In the room where he was sleeping another fire "erupted" in the blankets surrounding him and Claude Thibault. A sleeve of his cloak and part of his jacket was burned. He was awakened by smoke and the sight of Thibault extinguishing the flames.

This is a triumvirate of important information. What the homeowner and his servants have effectively done is connect Angélique to another fire. It is not a huge leap from this small fire to the flames that destroyed the lower town. The witnesses have also intertwined Claude Thibault in these possible misdeeds. There will undoubtedly be further efforts to find the former servant or have Angélique confess to his involvement. Those efforts will undoubtedly be painful for Angélique.

* * *

Two other witnesses come before Judge Raimbault today. They reaffirm information that has already been introduced into the official court record, and the affirmation adds a potentially deadly weight to the rendering of a verdict. Monsieur Gamelin in no uncertain terms tells the court Madame de Francheville intended to sell Angélique for 600 pounds of gunpowder. Once the ice in the St. Lawrence started to thaw, she planned to send her in one of the first boats heading to Québec. The sale, it was made

152

clear, was spurred by Madame de Francheville's fear of her slave. "She dared not, no longer having her maid, sleep alone in her house."

There is more. The merchant said his friend and business associate also told him three other things that are relevant: she had only left her house the day of the fire to attend church; Angélique had never served her well; and her servant left because of Angélique.

The final witness of the day is Jeanne Nafrechoux de Béréy. She shares what her Panis slave, Marie-Manon, shared with her. She blamed Angélique for setting the fire because she threatened that her mistress "would not laugh for long, that she would not sleep in her house."

Madame de Béréy further quoted her slave as saying that Angélique had behaved unusually. She repeatedly crossed the street; she stared in the direction of the de Francheville roof.

The implications are obvious. I wonder if they will be obvious to Angélique. She's up next.

* * *

We are moving to the city jail. There can be only one reason for the change of venue. Angélique will be interrogated.

Again.

                    * * *

Judge Raimbault starts where this all
started, with the fire. "Did the fire begin in
Lady de Francheville's house?"

Angélique says she does not know, but
she has something new to add, at least new
to me. When she went outside, the roof on
fire was nearest to Sieur Radisson's chimney.
If this is accurate, it means Angélique could
not have set the fire. But is it accurate? Is the
slave lying, or is she simply mistaken? I
make a note to follow up, although I am not
sure how I will do this.

Next, Judge Raimbault asks Angélique
where she was when Sieur Radisson tried to
douse the flames in Madame de
Francheville's home. Angélique's response
answers and evades the question. "I do not
know who went up first. I know that
someone went up calling for water as I stood
in the street."

I stop mid-sentence. This is a
contradiction. Angélique previously attested
she knew who appeared first to help fight the
fire: Sieur Radisson. Now she says she does
not know. This is an easy question, and an
easy answer to keep straight. I wonder why
the slave has changed her answer. I wonder
if she knows she has. I understand it is easy
to get confused when questions are being
tossed at you like the slings of an arrow. But
honesty should require no memory aid.

154

There is another reason why Angélique may have misspoke. Languishing in a jail cell no bigger than a horse stall, if that, eating crusts of bread, stale at best, must take a toll. Is this testimony the result of that toll? I will not share this with Madeleine.

The energy shift in the room is palpable. This may be because it is the accused speaking or it may be that the contradiction, seemingly as small as it is, indicates progress. Angélique is breaking.

Judge Raimbault continues his barrage of questions. He asserts Angélique threatened to burn down Madame de Francheville's house. The question he asks is long, full of reminders of words she is said to have spoken and the reason for her rancor.

Angélique's response is a simple denial.

We shift to the first fire. A finger of blame is pointed at her and her lover. Angélique dismisses the accusations. "The fire started on my blanket as I slept. The blanket touched the stove that was fiercely hot. The servant awoke me." As for Thibault, coincidentally his blanket also burned as a result of being too close to the fire, no doubt the result of his two sleep mates pushing the blanket toward the flames while they all slept.

I reread my hasty notes. I delete "coincidentally." It is sarcasm and it is editorializing. It is unfair. It is also what most people must surely be thinking.

But Angélique is not to be undone. Judge Raimbault pushes his point. "You are not telling the truth." The foundation for the falsehood, he says, is evident in the disappearance the next day of Angélique and Claude Thibault. The fire starts on Saturday night; they flee on Sunday.

The slave corrects his timeline. "The fire took place only on the night of Friday into Saturday. We left on Sunday at 7:30 in the evening."

The rest of the interrogation is spent on the escape, on where Angélique and Claude Thibault went after they ran from Monsieur Monière's house. Where they stayed and for how long. How long they had been planning their escape.

The plan, it would appear, had been in the works for some time.

* * *

We make our way out of the jail. Rolant is waiting for me. He thrusts a piece of paper in my hand. It is a petition from the prosecutor to recall witnesses and to have the accused confront those witnesses.

Confrontation is part of the judicial process. It enables the accused to deny accusations directly. It gives witnesses the opportunity to rethink, perhaps to revise, their earlier testimony.

"When?" I ask.

"Within the week."

We are running out of time to find new evidence and new witnesses, to determine without doubt what in the Lord's name actually happened the night of April 10.

"I will review my notes. Identify anything that could require follow up in light of today's testimony."

"That may have to wait until tomorrow." This is not Rolant speaking. It is Henri Geôlier. "There has been a new sighting of Claude Thibault. The police are calling on all available men to assist in the hunt."

I turn to Rolant. He nods. "Go."

* * *

We are among the last to arrive at the designated gathering area. We stopped first at home to let Madeleine know I would be late, perhaps very late, and to collect some warmer clothes and sustenance. Monsieur Geôlier strongly recommended the latter. "We will get hungry."

There are at least twenty of us. Many are police officers or military. A few, like me, work in law enforcement in some capacity. We are a motley crew. Those who have been on hunts before are prepared: clothing, boots, food, wine. The rest of us grabbed what we could, what we thought we would need. I am glad now for Monsieur Geôlier.

It is not yet mid-afternoon, and there is plenty of light to search easily. A tall man built like the side of a barn is speaking.

Giving orders without demanding or demeaning. We will work in groups of five. I am in Monsieur Geôlier's group. Each group will take a section of road and adjacent area and search. We will meet at the next gathering point a mile further down.

Our section of road is a ten-minute walk away. We move briskly. Our leader has informed us Claude Thibault was spotted in the vicinity last night. If he knows he was spotted, he will have made for the woods. If he is travelling primarily at night and sleeping during the day, he will make for the woods. We make for the woods.

We fan out in what Monsieur Geôlier calls a grid pattern. We do not want one of us to get lost or to wander off. It is slow going. I have my good boots on, but it does not take long for my legs and feet to become weary. Monsieur Geôlier says that is part excitement, part living in town. "You do not walk. You do not hunt. You do not farm."

He is right. I think of Acadie. Of being outdoors, working in the soil, the mud, the water of the Baie Française. At the end of the day, bones ached and muscles throbbed, but the body was content. So was the spirit.

Someone yells. They have found something. It is a cloth. Perhaps for around the neck, or to wipe away grime from hands and face. It does not look like it belongs to a woman, but we cannot know it belongs to Claude Thibault. We redouble our efforts.

Comb the area. Get down on hands and knees in some spots. We find nothing else.

We meet up with the other men at the next gathering spot. No one has located anything as definitive as our cloth. I feel a pride I cannot trace to its origin. Some groups have identified broken twigs below bird level and above animal height; some have seen markings in the earth, the mud, footprints perhaps.

We are buoyed by our discoveries as meagre as they are. We forge on to the next swathe of road and trees and the next gathering spot and the next. It is nearly evening. We have only a few hours left before the sun goes down. Our leader suggests we take ten minutes to rest and eat. Someone starts a fire. Someone else brings out a pot (I have no idea from where) and suddenly there is tea. It is the best tea I have ever tasted.

* * *

These are men who talk. These are men who voice their opinions without hesitation. And with assurance. I admire this assurance and realize these are not like the men who fill in the corners of my life: refined, educated, literate, well-heeled.

"You are sore, eh," laughs Monsieur Geôlier. He is not belittling me; he is helping me to feel part of the group.

"We are all sore," says another man. There is more laughter and agreement.

"The question is are we sore for nothing?" I do not know the speaker (I know none of the men here), but he has voiced what we are all thinking.

The answer, it appears, divides the group. Half of us want to continue the hunt, convinced Claude Thibault is out there under the trees waiting to be caught. The other half feel this is an exercise in futility.

"The man is not here. He was never here."

"He left the night of the fire. Got the hell out of town. That's what I'd do. That's what we'd all do."

"Unless we had a friend." This is Monsieur Geôlier. He has the attention of the group. He has my attention. "Monsieur Archambeau has sources that say the man may never have left Montréal."

Now I have everyone's attention. "There are those who say the safest thing to do was to stay put and wait until the furor has died down."

"But who would hide him? Who would take such a risk?" This is a question several of the men ask. I feel the eyes of our leader on me.

"It would be a woman," says the jailer. "Claude Thibault was always bragging about his women."

The men laugh. This is what men do, yes, they show how virile they are to other men.

"I heard he slept with the Black slave every day."

"I heard he slept with any slave."

"I heard he slept with any woman."

"That explains the baby."

Heads turn toward the last speaker. "My wife's cousin has a daughter who works as a servant in one of the houses on rue Saint-Paul. She says another servant was with child. With Claude Thibault's child."

"All the more reason to leave," says another man. Everyone laughs. I find myself joining in.

"So, we have gossip and insinuation. What we do not have is Thibault." This is our leader. He is correct. We are wasting time. As enjoyable as I find the time has been.

* * *

Madeleine is waiting up for me. It is late, very late, when we finally get home. My wife has a cold plate of food and a hot pot of coffee ready. She tilts her head as I walk in the door. I shake my head "no." I am amazed at how we communicate without words, the ease with which we know what the other is asking, and saying.

"Was it awful?"

"It was not," I admit. "It has been a long time since I have been with a group of men comfortable in their skin and in the natural environment. It felt good."

I have spoken without thinking. On the heels of embracing our ability to speak sans words, I have opened my mouth and expelled words that carry the slings of arrows. "You miss your home." Madeleine smiles, but sadness sits in the corners of her mouth.

"This is my home," I remind her. "I am exactly where I want to be."

My wife moves closer to me. I take her in my arms. I feel the weight of her worry and a baby in her womb.

Chapter 15
Interrogation
Friday, May 7, 1734

Things are moving ahead quickly. And slowly. Shortly after I am settled at my desk, papers spread before me, Rolant arrives with another piece of paper. It is a judgment to file a writ against Claude Thibault.

The judgment states that Thibault is accused of setting fire to Madame de Francheville's house and, thereby, causing much of the lower town to burn. It also notes Angélique has disavowed any involvement, and the bailiffs have come up empty handed. Over the next two weeks, a public cry will ring out to summons Thibault. His possessions will be seized.

It will all be for naught.

I do not say this out loud, but my superior, as if reading my mind, agrees. "It must be done. No stone unturned."

"We combed those woods last night. He was not there, if he was ever there."

"I fear Thibault will not be found. I doubt he is even in New France. But the hunt is better than the alternative."

The alternative is torture.

* * *

We are talking about the writ. There is no need to keep this information confidential. The writ is a public document. Admittedly, not one Madeleine or Sidonie would likely come across during their day, but public nonetheless.

"What does it all mean?" Madeleine asks.

"It means Thibault is in big trouble. The only thing that can help him now would be to come forward."

"Why would he ever do that?" Sidonie wants to know. "You have already determined he is guilty."

It is an astute observation. There is, however, merit in the assumption of guilt. Would an innocent man flee? Would an innocent man remain in hiding? The answer to both questions is "no." I explain this. I do not get the endorsement I expected.

"Perhaps there is more than one justice," my wife says. "One for people who are white and wealthy, another for those who aren't."

I am aghast at the thought. (I am also a little concerned it may be blasphemous.) I reiterate the foundation on which the judicial system is based: a trial is a tenet of that system.

My wife points out another tenet of the system: if you are accused, you are presumed guilty.

"But how can it be otherwise?" I ask. "After an investigation, after speaking with witnesses an accused is identified, charged."

"Angélique was accused by the town crier while the street still blazed," says Sidonie. Her tone is polite, even deferential. The point she is making is neither.

"Tell me," I say, looking first at one woman and then the other, "why would you not turn yourself in if there was an arrest warrant out for you?"

My wife answers. "Because, perhaps, as an indentured servant in a country not his, Thibault does not trust the system."

"Instead, he hangs a woman he is supposed to love out to dry."

There is no response. Somehow in defending Thibault the defenders of Angélique have momentarily forgotten about the slave.

"What happens now?" Sidonie asks.

In less than a week, I tell them, we will be back in court. Angélique will face her accusers.

"What will that accomplish?" Madeleine asks.

"There are two likely outcomes. Either the accused confesses in the face of overwhelming evidence, or the witnesses change their mind."

"Angélique could go free?" This is Sidonie. I do not know if she is delighted at this thought or horrified by it.

I do not answer the question. Instead, I tell them about the hunt for Thibault, about the conversation over wine. Now there is no doubt, Sidonie is horrified. So is Madeleine.

"This is just men talking," I assure them. "There is no merit in the conversation. It is as the hunt leader said, merely gossip and insinuation."

"Still," says Sidonie quietly, "to so easily tarnish a man's reputation."

"Do not worry about that," I respond, "Thibault's reputation is already ruined."

"And," I add a little unkindly, "what does he care about reputation? He cannot even bother to come forward and defend himself."

* * *

May 10, 1734

Cher Maman, Papa,

Spring has arrived in Montréal. The evenings are starting to lengthen. The sun's rays are getting stronger. The breeze carries a hint of warmth and the light aroma of wood hyacinths. There is, as always, the infernal mud. I swear I spend more time cleaning my boots than wearing them.

Still, it is pleasant to walk without scurrying from wind and snow. Without feeling the chill of the day in your bones. It

166

is better for Madeleine, too. She can move less encumbered, take a moment to breathe in the scented air and relax.

I imagine you are readying the fields for crops, the garden for vegetables. You'll be repairing and bolstering the dykes. Mud that has a purpose. I think of you often and wish I was there to help.

The trial continues, but it is quiet at the moment. That will not last. Angélique will be given an opportunity, and soon, to respond to her accusers. This is as the law demands. This is only right.

I do not know how she will fare when face to face with the men and women who have said she threatened her owner and started a fire that destroyed the lower town. And it is destroyed. The streets are black with grime and ash. The heavy smell of smoke lingers yet. Walking is precarious; the eyes assaulted by the remnants of what were once beautiful houses and thriving businesses.

In the midst of such loss, I am ashamed of my happiness. Undoubtedly, Madeleine and I are happy. We have a loving home, food on the table, and the freedom to move about as we wish. The baby is doing well. I think she will be an excellent dancer. (Tomorrow, I will be convinced the baby is a "he.")

I know you are as happy as we are. The land is good, and the Lord provides. We are blessed.

Your loving son,
Philippe

PS Madeleine sends her love. Le bébé
aussi.

Chapter 16
Confrontation
Wednesday, May 12, 1734

The last few days have been a blur and a slow drip. The hours sped by; the minutes dragged on. We have been waiting for today. We have been waiting for the confrontation, for Angélique to come face to face with her accusers: friends, neighbours, owner.

Somehow this seems like dénouement, as if everything has been leading up to this moment. I know the wheels of justice will continue to turn in the wake of whatever happens today, but there is a finality about this. Perhaps it is the waiting, perhaps it is the body of evidence (or hearsay) that is already out there on the street being picked up and casually tossed around for conversational banter. Perhaps it is that I am reaching my own conclusions, and it is time to stop wavering.

Confrontation is a central part of the justice system in New France. It, we are proud to say, gives accuser and accused the opportunity to come together, to speak to one another, to deny, to admit, to change testimony. It is not a pleasant process. The accused must listen to others point a finger of blame, besmirch their reputation, say unkind things. The accusers must have their testimony questioned, refuted, rejected. Both sides will be called liars, and worse.

It is, undoubtedly, the most exciting part of the trial.

* * *

The afternoon starts off, as much in the legal system does, on a routine note. Five witnesses come forward. Their testimony is read, and each agrees that what they had said was truthful. There are no changes. The last of these witnesses, Marie-Manon, adds to her testimony. She identifies a new, albeit unknown, witness. The de Béréy slave had previously said she saw Angélique looking up toward the roof of the de Francheville house. Now, she adds, she went at this time to stand against the courtyard wall of the Hôtel-Dieu. There was a recovering soldier there, one with a bandaged hand. "He could see Angélique as well as I could."

* * *

Marie-Manon has a bigger role to play today than enhancing her testimony. She is the first to confront Angélique. Preliminaries aside, the Panis slave's testimony is read to Angélique in its entirety. Angélique's response is simple and vehement: "You are wretched, untruthful, and unworthy."

I cannot tell if the malice has disconcerted Marie-Manon. She appears calm. It may be that she anticipated this response, and she certainly knows Angélique. The spite is not unexpected. Marie-Manon quietly reaffirms that her deposition is truthful.

Angélique contends it is not. "I did not say that my mistress will not long be in her home and will not sleep there. I did not cross to the other side of the street and look toward the roof of the house."

She does agree with some of what Marie-Maon has to say. At five in the afternoon on the day of the fire, she was playing with the Panis slave. Their game involved crossing the street. There was a man in the door of the hospital, but he was not a soldier, rather a man named Latreille from Québec who has been staying at the Hôtel-Dieu for many months.

Marie-Manon agrees and disagrees. It is the timeline she calls into question.

It is clear there are grains of truth here. Equally clear: neither woman is backing down.

* * *

My audience is rapt. Madeleine and Sidonie are hanging on my every word. I quite like it. Sadly, the topic is not a happy one. It is a recap of today's events. I try to stick to the facts but find myself adding commentary.

"What does it all mean? Who cares whether the bandaged man was a soldier or from Québec?" Sidonie finally asks when I stop for breath and a sip of tea.

We are, as usual, sitting in the garden of the Hôtel-Dieu. If it were not for the circumstances that have brought us here, this would be pleasant. From the outside perhaps, it looks like friends or neighbours having a conversation in the early hours of the evening.

Sidonie's question gets to the heart of the confrontation. Angélique has had an opportunity to confront the first of her accusers. Has it made any difference? Likely not. Will it make any difference moving forward? That will depend on whether Angélique or her accusers change their story in any significant way.

"Is that likely?"

I turn to my wife and shrug. "The slave is resolute, but there are starting to be the smallest alterations in the story she has woven for the court. That may be her undoing."

"Why?" Sidonie's question is simple and fundamental. Madeleine answers it.

"Because the court assumes you have only one memory, and it never falters."

I look into my teacup. That was a little harsh, but it was not inaccurate. "We believe there is truth in consistency. We also recognize, however, that in the heat of the moment, in the hours following tragedy, we may not remember all the details of what we witnessed. That is why everyone is given an opportunity to have their testimony read back to them. It is why we challenge that testimony."

'What about Claude Thibault?"

"Nothing has changed Sidonie. He is still wanted. He remains at large."

"You think he is gone for good." Madeleine looks directly at me. She has not voiced this thought before. Perhaps it is only now occurring to her.

"I think he may have hidden here for a while, but that time has passed. I do not believe Claude Thibault is in New France."

"I think that is for the best," my wife says. Sidonie nods her agreement.

Chapter 17
Confrontation
Thursday, May 13, 1734

Henri Geôlier is halfway through my lunch. "Today was a bust, eh."

Not the most loquacious of statements, but accurate, nonetheless. Six witnesses. Nothing new.

This tells me two things. First, that Monsieur Geôlier eavesdrops. I am not surprised. Second, that the nuances of what he hears behind closed doors is not lost on him. I am not surprised.

"Six witnesses, six people saying their original deposition is correct and truthful."

That is not quite accurate. The sixth and final witness, Jeanne de la Baume made a potential amendment. She said she was not sure whether Angélique said she would cut her mistress's throat or motioned the action of cutting someone's throat.

"It will not make a difference."

Monsieur Geôlier is right. The intent of the statement, verbal or otherwise, is evident and resolute. Angélique threatened to harm her mistress. From what we have learned so far, that animus is not atypical. Indeed, it appears to be the norm.

* * *

There is a steady stream of rain falling from the sky to the earth. The result: more

Montréal mud. It oozes from doorways, from street corners, from the hems of skirts and pants. Madeleine and I have wisely decided to stay in tonight. We will see Sidonie tomorrow when the mud has baked into a dirty brown powder that adheres to skin, nostrils, clothes.

A bright, warm fire is burning. The evening dishes are cleaned and returned to their proper spot. I am sitting before the flames reading. Madeleine is stitching. We are content. Part of that contentment may be the pact we made over dinner: no talk tonight about arson or the woman who is on trial for arson. We are giving ourselves what Angélique will unlikely never get in her lifetime: the right to choose how we spend our time.

Conversation is sporadic, but there is no awkwardness here. This is the ease that comes with being comfortable in someone's presence. There is no artifice, only acceptance.

There is, however, a chill in the air. The fire has started to die. Smoke begins to seep across the floor. Madeleine and I are on our feet at the same time. She moves a log so it is more centrally positioned in the hearth. I bend down to help. The log is charred black on one end, barely burned on the other.

Madeleine sees my look of surprise. "This is common. The fire burned more intensely under one end of the log. Easily fixed."

It is not the log that has me mesmerized. It is the image of the wooden shingle I found in rue Saint-Paul a lifetime ago.

Chapter 18
Confrontation
Friday, May 14, 1734

The three shingles are lying on my desk. Not saying a word. I have been staring at them for thirty minutes now. Nothing. Well, that is not quite true. Nothing more than what they had been saying all along had I deigned to look more closely and consider what they were telling me.

It is the first shingle that has the most to say. Almost intact. Blackened heavily on one end. Another slash of black a third of the way along. A similar slash near the end of the wood. This wood did not burn evenly. Not all wood does, of course. But the thick ebony char indicates one thing. The same thing Madeleine so causally pointed out last night as she rearranged the logs in the hearth.

The fire started here.

"Getting low on wood?"

It is Rolant's attempt at humor. In my reverie, I did not hear him come up behind me. I jump. He laughs. Then he sees my face.

"What are we looking at?"

"Shingles from the fire."

"We have seen these before."

He's right. I have seen these before, but I wasn't looking at what was right in front of me. "Last night at home a log started to smoke. Caught in fire at one end."

"The point of origin."

I nod. I also see Rolant's confusion. "This shingle isn't from the de Francheville house. It's from the de Béréy house."

"What are you saying?" I hear the thud as Rolant's body lands in my chair.

* * *

We are at another impasse. Marguerite César is back in court. The neighbour who kept a close eye on Angélique the night of the fire attests to the veracity of her testimony. Angélique says in so many words, "So what?"

The slave points out she had a habit of moving about. She was often in the street.

Not like this, responds Madame César. "I had never seen her watching so attentively for so long as she had been doing in the street. This is what caused me to worry. This is what made me go outside to see what was causing her to look from side to side."

* * *

Angélique is once again on her own. This is the fourth interrogation. It is five o'clock. The skies are heavy with cloud and a threat of rain hovers in the air. The chamber off the prison where we are gathered feels like the lull before the storm. Foreboding what is to come.

The focus is on Thibault, he of the elusive whereabouts. The information, however, is new to the court. It is not new to Rolant or to me, thanks to the jailer who enjoys my lunch each day.

"On the day you were placed in prison, did Claude Thibault not bring you supper? What did he say to you?"

As with her previous responses today, Angélique's testimony is to the point. Claude Thibault did not bring me supper. She did not speak with him. She saw him only in the morning of the day she was apprehended. He was in the courtyard of the Hôtel-Dieu, but they did not speak.

It is hard to read Judge Raimbault. I am sure this seeming detachment has been honed over years. He switches gears as easily as shifting from one foot to the other. "Where were you when you spoke to the injured man, Latreille, slightly prior to the fire being noticed?"

"I was at the door of Madame de Francheville's house. Latreille was at the entrance of the hospital yard."

"Is it not true that you went up the stairs of the house while the girls were playing in the yard after supper?"

"I did not go up the staircase. The girls were not at play in the yard, but on the contrary, in the street."

"What was the name of the sentry who stood at the door of the Hôtel-Dieu courtyard or garden during the night when Thibault entered there?"

The question comes out of nowhere. I make a note to check up on the sentry and his whereabouts the night of the fire and subsequently. Angélique sems unphased. She gives a lengthy answer that relies on specific details. "The man named La Ruine, gardener at the hospital, called the sentry La Riviere. He told Thibault he could warm himself at the sentry station."

The interrogation is over. We are at an impasse.

* * *

The day ends with Françoise Geoffrion. The neighbourhood servant had previously told the court she met Angélique early on the afternoon of the fire and asked Angélique if she was having a quiet stroll and still with Madame de Francheville. The slave told her she had little time to stroll and that she would not be living with her mistress for much longer.

Angélique wears her apparent nonchalance like a mantle. "There is no harm in that. Knowing that my mistress had sent away her servant but for a given time and that she had said she had sold me and written to the intendant on this matter, I could indeed reply as I did."

Impasse.

* * *

We are walking to the lower town. I think we are comfortably meandering. Madeliene senses something else. "You are eager to see Sidonie tonight." My wife is right. And wrong.

I do want to speak with Sidonie more than usual, but it is not eagerness; it is anxiety. I must ask her about the shingle. The context of the shingle.

Sidonie has tea ready. She wants to hear about the trial, the confrontation. I give her what little there is to give. She is disappointed. Perhaps confused. I share both sentiments with her.

"Does this never end?"

"Soon it will be in the past, but it will take us some more time to get there. Justice cannot be rushed." This last pronouncement is not met with the reverence I believe it deserves, but I understand how difficult it is for those outside the system to appreciate its processes and the need for each and every step.

"What is Angélique like?" Sidonie wants to know. "Does she cry?"

"She does not cry. Not yet anyway," I say. "I do not know that she will. She holds her own. There is a dignity to her stance."

"You sound like you admire her?" My wife says this with approval. Sidonie looks as

181

if someone has told her women should wear pants.

"The confrontation, in particular, is hard. There is animosity. Sides are divided. Angélique sounds reasonable in her responses, not emotional."

"Do you think she is lying?" my wife asks.

"I do not think she is completely honest, and her story is not always consistent. There is not, however, the obvious fabrication, the tumbling of words that signal untruth."

"What will happen now?" Sidonie asks.

"More of the same, and they will keep on her about Claude Thibault."

"Why?" Sidonie asks. "Why can't they just leave that alone and give Angélique some peace."

It is not a question. I answer it anyway. "The justice system is not about giving anyone peace."

* * *

We sip our tea in silence for a few minutes. I would like to say it is a companionable silence. I do not know that it is.

"Sidonie, could you tell me where you were when the fire started?"

The servant looks at me askance. There are likely a number of reasons for her incredulity. I ignore the look and its implications. "Monsieur, I have answered this question a dozen times."

"Yes," I acknowledge with appreciation, "you have. I am working some things out in my mind, and it will be helpful to review the sequence of events. I am hoping you will not mind helping."

What can she say? Now it is my wife who looks at me askance. I ignore that look as well, but I may pay for that disregard later. Ignorance is not bliss.

"I do not know where I was when the fire started. I know where I was when someone first yelled, 'Fire!'"

It is a distinction with merit, and one, interestingly, that several witnesses have made. Angélique herself has noted the important line that separates the two.

"Tell me." There is no judgment here. A simple request.

"I was in the house when I heard someone call out "Fire!"

"Was it Angélique?"

"I believed it was at the time, at least in the days following the fire. I no longer know. Does it matter?"

It always come back to this: the question of relevance. It is a question I cannot answer. Not now anyway. Not without a complete picture.

"Did you see the fire?" Madeleine and Sidonie look at me in shock. It is my wife who shows me the error of my question.

"Everyone saw the fire Philippe."

"Yes, yes. Of course. I meant the start of the fire. After the first yell but before everyone arrived to help."

Sidonie is thinking about her answer. This is a sign of commitment to accuracy. I am pleased.

"When I heard the yell, I ran outside. I looked up. The roof was on fire."

"What roof?"

The shock is back. This time it is quickly accompanied by unexpected insight. The women know what I am really asking.

"You do not think the fire started in the de Francheville house?" Sidonie has put into words what I have been afraid to say even to myself.

"No, no." My denial is quick. This is strategy and protection. "I am trying to confirm exactly what people saw and when. The fire spread rapidly. What you observed will help me understand the sequence of events."

This explanation will appease Sidonie. It will not appease my wife. I may be in for a long night. I fear it may get even longer with my next question. I turn to Sidonie.

"Where was Marie-Manon when the fire started?"

Chapter 19
Confrontation
Saturday, May 15, 1734

There is a new witness. Rolant forewarns me before I enter the chamber room. I must be on my toes.

"Judge Raimbault is not to be underestimated," says Rolant. "The unexpected questions have purpose. You will see that today."

The first witness, the new witness, is Louis Bellefeuille dit La Ruine, the gardener of the Hôtel-Dieu. He whose name came up in the question about the sentry, as I'm sure Judge Raimbault knew it would.

Monsieur La Ruine modestly says he knows nothing then proceeds to tell us what he does know: Claude Thibault was eating a meal at the table set out for those in need the night of the fire. "I told him I was surprised to find him calmly eating supper while the fire was everywhere. To which he replied that he was hungry having found himself spent and having not yet eaten that day."

The gardener goes on to say that someone arrived with a jar of eau de vie that was drunk by many people present. Someone else paid for more liquor, and

Angélique offered up syrup from a bottle. The offer did not appease Monsieur La Ruine. He accused the slave of starting the fire. Her response?

"You would think me quite daft to set fire to where we live."

Still not appeased, Monsieur La Ruine accused Angélique once more. Her response. Silence.

* * *

The first confrontation of the day pits Angélique against Marie-Louise Poirier, the servant who left the de Francheville home rather than continue to work with the slave. Here there is animosity. At the very least outright disagreement.

Immediately out of the gate, Angélique denies much of what the servant has to say.

> *She did not forbid me to drink eau de vie.*
> *She is a true liar.*
> *She has no authority to forbid me to go out. I do not have to ask permission of anyone.*
> *I went out as I wished.*

Some things she clarifies.

> *I stole no deerskins when I fled with Claude Thibault. We*

got those from a man named des Custeaux for six francs in silver that I had brought from New England when I was sent by Nichus Block to the now deceased Sieur Francheville.

I never stated that if I could ever return to my country and there were whites there, I would have them burned like dogs wherever possible. There is little wrong in me stating that the French are of little worth.

Jean Joseph Laflamendiere, the surgeon, is up next but has nothing new to offer the proceedings.

It is more of the same. The next few days, I fear, may repeat the pattern again and again.

Chapter 20
Confrontation
Monday, May 17, 1734

May 17, 1734

Cher Maman, Papa,

You would not know it from today, but, I believe, the end is in sight. I do not know if I feel that way because the scales are so heavily tilted in one direction or because we cannot continue on this path indefinitely. In the absence of a confession, in the absence of naming a co-conspirator, Judge Raimbault continues to seek new witnesses and reaffirm existing testimony.

Today there were two confrontations. More of the same. Angélique (I thought quite adroitly) dismissed one of the implications inherent in Louis Traversy's testimony. Madame de Francheville's tenant farmer had sworn the slave said she would not leave tracks in the snow next time. Angélique contended he misspoke. Rather, she said she was imprudent not to wait for the snow to be gone when she first fled; had she waited her footsteps would have gone unseen. Angélique also denied ever calling her mistress a "whore."

Monsieur Traversy was having none of the rewording of his words. He said his version of the conversation was correct.

It was Angélique, however, who I feel got the final thrust. "My poor Traversy, you could be speaking erroneously."

Monsieur Traversy's wife, Marie-Françoise Thomelet, was the second and final witness of the day. She is much like her husband. Angélique dismissed her accusations as simply and unceremoniously as she had her husband's. "My poor Thomelet, I did not say at all that I would have my mistress burned."

Madame Thomelet was not easily dismissed. She looked at Angélique and said her recounting was accurate. She said they were together gutting pigs on the eve of Saint Thomas, and she warned the slave if she continued to be malevolent her mistress would sell her. We heard once again, Angélique's response: If she sells me, I will have her burned or torched. This was followed by the farmer's wife cautioning the slave that such behaviour would result in her death by hanging. Angélique's response to the farmer's wife: "to snigger and spring in her seat."

Angélique's response to the farm woman's testimony today. "Madame Thomelet is wretched to state as much, that it is not the truth."

My poor Maman, Papa, you asked to hear about my day, about the trial, my work. I fear now I have worn you out with details you did not desire. I send my apologies. And my devotion.

Your loving son,
Philippe

PS Le bébé is getting ready to welcome the world. Madeleine is as round as a little pumpkin, la citrouille, although I do not tell her this.

Chapter 21
Confrontation
Wednesday, May 19, 1734

"Your girl is not doing well, eh." Henri Geôlier is halfway through my lunch. He shares this insight with me as casually as I now share my loaf of bread and plate of ham.

"What do you mean?"

"What part confused you?" The jailer finds his joke so funny he stops chewing and slaps his hand on my desk.

"I thought she did well in court."

"That may be. She is not doing well in gaol."

"Does anyone do well in gaol?"

"Touché."

* * *

It is a lovely spring evening. The sun is out. The breeze warm. The insects have taken the night off. Madeleine and I should be talking about baby names and clothes and what we will do together as a family of three. Instead, we are discussing Angélique. To be honest, I am tired of talking about Angélique. And still....

"Surely that must not surprise you." My wife is referring to Monsieur Geôlier's comment.

"It does surprise me. In court, she holds her own."

"Or is it that you want to see her holding her own?" My face reveals my reaction. I had not considered this. I am the special rapporteur, and I had not considered this.

There is softness now in Madeleine's voice. She does not mean to be hurtful. "Logic tells us no one fares well in gaol. The cell is smaller than a wooden wardrobe. There is barely room to lie flat. Food is scarce and substandard. Hard crusts of bread, moldy. There are vermin of all shapes and sizes, and no human interaction to speak of. I am surprised Angélique is still standing."

My mouth is hanging open. My wife reaches over and gently closes it. "How do you know all this?"

Madeleine smiles. "The women in the neighbourhood talk, the people at the Hôtel-Dieu talk. But mostly I learned all this from you."

I really must stop discussing Angélique.

* * *

That goal will have to wait until tomorrow to be attained. We are here in the courtyard of the Hôtel-Dieu. There is still a small group of people looking for a meal and a place to stay. There will always be a group of people looking for a meal and a place to stay. Sometimes the group will not be small. The sisters always accommodate.

Tonight, they share their tea with us as they do every night. Those who come are welcomed. Madeleine can sense my discomfort. She guides the conversation but does not shy away from what we have learned from Monsieur Geôlier.

"It must be terrible for her."

"Gaol is supposed to be terrible." This does not come out the way I had intended.

"How much longer will they keep her in this awful place?"

"Not much longer I fear." This also does not come out the way I had intended. Both women give me a look: one is withering, the other aghast.

"It is not a night for good news, this night. I would like to talk of wildflowers and walks, sunshine, and babies about to be born, but we have at this table committed ourselves to honesty, and I will be honest with you." Sidonie has lowered her head. She does not want to hear what I have to say. Madeleine's face is raised. She meets my eyes. Her eyes tell me she does not want to hear what I have to say.

"Judge Raimbault will not wait much longer."

"Much longer to what?" Sidonie asks.

"Much longer to render a verdict."

"But how can he render a verdict in the absence of definitive proof?" Madeleine seems surprised at this, and saddened.

"Definitive proof can be elusive. You make the best decision you can based on the evidence you have."

"The judge does not have much evidence." Madeleine tries to sound hopeful.

"That is wishful thinking. Judge Raimbault has gone above and beyond. He has interviewed more than a dozen witnesses – closer to two dozen – and interviewed them again. He has interrogated and confronted the accused on four separate occasions. He is to be applauded."

"And still Angélique has not confessed. She has not given up Claude Thibault."

Sidonie looks up hopefully. I am about to dash that hope. "So, what do you think will now happen next?"

This is unfair of me, unfair and mean. I love one of these women; the other has been nothing but helpful. It is the other who is the first to interpret my meaning. Sidonie looks at me with horror.

"Mais non, the brodequins."

Chapter 22
Confrontation
Wednesday, May 26, 1734

A week has passed. There has been no further discussion of torture. At least, with Madeleine or Sidonie. Rolant and I have also stayed away from the topic, but it hovers over the work we do. We have reviewed, and reviewed again, our notes. We do not believe we have missed anything. I have spoken, again, with the merchants, servants, suppliers, and soldiers who informed my initial research. As with the witnesses, there has been no substantive change in their stories, no additional information outside the odd detail or two.

It is the shingle that has us perplexed. Given its location, the reasonable conclusion is that the fire did not start in the de Francheville home, but next door. We weigh this conclusion against the evidence presented in court and the research I have undertaken. The reasonable conclusion is that the fire had to start in the de Francheville home.

We dismiss the disconnect with a myriad of explanations.

The shingle did not fall straight down; it was carried by the wind.

There was a second blast when nearby shingles caught fire, hence, the unusual pattern.

Someone kicked or moved the shingle to a new location on the ground.

Most shingles look like this. We just didn't see most of the shingles after the fire.

We put the shingle and our discomfort aside. There will be more witnesses and confrontations today. Perhaps we will learn something new.

We will soon discover there is no need for alternate explanations or additional insight. Things are about to solidify and fall apart. For the court and the slave, respectively.

* * *

It should come as no surprise, and yet it does. The chief prosecutor François Foucher makes a formal application to the court.

I request on behalf of the King that it be ordained that prior to rendering the

*final trial judgement, the
accused be subjected to
torture in the ordinary and
extraordinary ways, and
interrogated on the facts of
the trial, and once her
interrogation done and
communicated to me, I will
determine what is
required.*

* * *

There is no time to mull over the implications of the request. There is also no need. The request makes it clear the court does not believe it can get a confession from Angélique without resorting to torture. There is no doubt in anyone's mind a confession is now within reach.

First though, the trial must progress as trials progress. I expect more of the same. I am wrong.

The sole witness is Amable Lemoine Monière. She is four or five years old and, I presume in hindsight, has no idea the fury she is about to unleash. The little girl says she was playing with Madame de Francheville's niece and another child when the fire started. She says she was sitting at the door to the house when she saw Angélique taking embers in a shovel up to the attic.

The silence in the room is deafening.

* * *

There is no comfort in the warmth of the evening sun or the hot tea tonight. It is as if the three of us sitting round a small table in the courtyard of the Hôtel-Dieu have come to an unspoken realization that simultaneously saddens us and unites us.

The end is in sight.

Madeleine asks me, not for the first time, if I believe the little girl. I have no reason not to. She did not seem coached or ill at ease (any more ill at ease than a young girl would who is seated in a strange room and questioned by a judge).

"Why are we only hearing this now?" Sidonie wants to know. It is a good question. But it is not as flush with conspiracy as we might think.

"It is likely no one questioned the little girl. Or they asked her about the fire and where she was when it started. This is before the fire. My guess, and this is common with children, they do not connect the dots. Embers in a shovel and fire in the street are worlds apart."

"Not for Angélique," my wife points out.

"Not for any of us," I respond. What the little girl had to say will carry a big weight when it comes to assessing guilt and innocence.

There is really only one thing left to discuss, and it is Madeleine who opens the door to the conversation. "You must tell us."

"It is not pleasant."

"None of this is pleasant."

I understand what the two women want to know without putting explicit words to their question. I give them the answer they are dreading. "The court will render a verdict. That verdict will not satisfy if there is no confession. If Angélique does not admit she started the fire, she will be tortured.

Chapter 23
Confrontation
Thursday, May 27, 1734

Dawn has broken. The early morning sun holds out hope for a warm day with more to follow. We need the promise of summer. As I walk to work, I reflect on the months ahead: there will be a new baby; there will be no more need for a special rapporteur.

The court is convening early. It is six o'clock, and the first confrontation is about to start. It will pit Charlotte Trottier Desrivières, the ten-year-old who was playing in the street with Madame de Francheville's niece, against Angélique. This is an elemental clash: privilege versus oppression, child versus adult. I wonder absently if it was difficult for the young girl to get up this morning. If she is scared. Then I wonder the same thing about Angélique.

The musings are irrelevant. Both of them are here, at the ready, at the will of the court.

There is the predictable preamble: an oath to tell the truth, a statement acknowledging the two people know one another, a reading of the original deposition. There is the predictable denial from

Angélique: she did not see Charlotte playing in the yard; she did not go up to the attic; the other witness, young Amable did not see her go upstairs either because Angélique was sitting with her on the stoop watching the other girls play. There is the predictable affirmation of the original testimony: Charlotte says she played with Marguerite de Couagne; she says Amable was at the stoop; she says Amable said, "There is Angélique;" she heard someone go up the staircase.

I am writing furiously. The predictable has become the unexpected. I make two notes. Did Angélique ever say she was sitting on the stoop with Amable before today? Did young Charlotte ever say she heard Amable reference Angélique before today?

As I write, pushing shock and disbelief into the recesses of my mind, places where a special rapporteur does not travel, I applaud Judge Raimbault. This is why you interrogate and interrogate again. This is why you confront. Stories change. The question is why? That question will become paramount with the next witness.

* * *

We are back where this all began, with Étienne Volant Radisson, the very first witness in the trial of Marie-Joseph Angélique. It is now six-thirty in the morning.

Angélique corrects Sieur Radisson's testimony. She says she did not alert him about the fire; she did not climb the staircase or go to the attic with him or anyone else; she remembers seeing only one person while she was at the door to the street.

Sieur Radisson is having none of this. He speaks with what I feel is authority and assurance. He contends, as he has from the outset, that Angélique ran to him saying, "Monsieur, there is a fire at the house of Madame de Francheville." In response, he grabbed two pails of water, ran to the house, climbed the stairs to the attic and the pigeon loft. There was no ladder to climb further.

I should be writing furiously. Instead, I sit stock-still. This contradicts what Angélique said earlier. It was pivotal testimony then; it is pivotal testimony now. And it is not what Angélique originally said was the truth.

* * *

There is no time to dissect this new information, this changed information. It must be done, but it will be done later. It is eight o'clock and it is time for the last witness. Young Amable Lemoine Monière is here to confront Angélique with all of the rigor and aplomb a young child can muster.

The confrontation is anticlimactic. Perhaps it was destined to be. A five-year-old pitted against a twenty-nine-year-old. The innocence of youth versus the proclaimed innocence of an adult fighting for her life. There is no winning here.

I remind myself this is not about winning; it is about justice. It is as if Angélique comes to understand she cannot disavow the memories of a child. First, she accuses Amable of telling falsehoods. Then she says someone must have told the young girl to say she took embers to the attic. Then she turns to the girl. "My little Amable, come here by me, and tell me who it is that told you to say this. I will give you a morsel of sugar."

Amable sticks to her story, the offer of candy apparently rejected. *You went upstairs while the little girls played.*

* * *

The chamber is crowded. Today Judge Raimbault is joined by four counsellors, all notaries and all of whom have been provided with the details of the trial to date. The room feels heavy with judgment.

There are a series of questions thrust at Angélique, repeated from previous interrogations: When did Madame de Francheville leave her house the day of the fire? For how long was she gone? When were the girls playing in the yard? Were fires burning in the chimneys of the house? Who came to the house the day of the fire? When did Claude Thibault enter the house?

And we are back to him again. The man who has seemingly disappeared from the face of the earth continues to play a key role in the trial of his lover. Angélique reiterates her previous testimony. She only saw Thibault when he helped remove possessions from the house after the fire started. She denied making plans to run away with him or anyone else.

Judge Raimbault is not going to let this line of questioning dissipate. I make a note. Perhaps I am missing something. He inquires why Angélique asked where Thibault was when she was brought to gaol. Same answer. He asks what she said to Thibault when he came to get his clothes from the gaol. Same answer. He asks what he brought her to eat. Same answer.

Judge Raimbault abruptly leaves Thibault behind. He moves, again, to the origin of the fire. Angélique seems composed, but I feel an undercurrent. It may be of my own making. She says, again, that she does not know the origin of the fire, if it started inside or outside. She also points out that she could have accurately stated there was no fire in any of the chimneys. What was there was so small as to be inconsequential.

Now we are back to Sieur Radisson. I lean forward. "I did not go to the house of Sieur Radisson and did not go up at all with him in the staircase, nor to the attic."

This statement is challenged. Judge Raimbault is blunt. The slave, he says, "is disguising the truth." On May 3rd she admitted Sieur Radisson had gone up with her to the said attic carrying two pails of water. Later she said she did not know at all who had gone up first to the attic because she was in the street at the time.

Angélique stays the course, the alternate course. "I do not know if Sieur Radisson went up to the attic. I did not see him at all. Indeed, I saw no one go up to the attic with pails of water. I only heard a call for water."

When asked where she was when the fire began, Angélique says she was at the doorway speaking to a man on the other side of the street at the Hôtel-Dieu. It was this man, she says, who let out a cry of "Fire!"

Now we move to another fire. The fire at Sieur Monière's house just prior to Angélique's escape with Claude Thibault. Judge Raimbault asks if she did not beg a servant in the house to tell Sieur Monière nothing of the fire. Angélique admits she did. "I begged the servant to say nothing of it for fear of Sieur Monière's outburst of rage as he had risen from his bed to the smell of smoke and gone upstairs with his son, lantern in hand."

I am trying not to pick sides. At times, I admire Judge Raimbault's dexterity and the details he extracts. Now, I think Angélique's answer makes perfect sense. If I were a slave sleeping in a stranger's house, would I not want to keep the fire a secret.

And where there is fire, there is Claude Thibault. Judge Raimbault asks two more questions related to the missing man. *The night you begged the servant was it the same night fire broke out downstairs where Thibault was sleeping? Why did you forbid Thibault from working for the commissioner?*

Angélique corrects the judge with respect to his first question. She says the downstairs fire broke out after the owner of the house had been awakened and made his rounds. With respect to the second question, her response made perfect sense. If her lover was working for someone, he could not have fled with her.

Another abrupt shift. Judge Raimbault pushes back about the inconsistency in Angélique's testimony, specifically about the little girls playing in the yard. One time she says, the little ones were not playing in the yard. Today, she says they were.

Angélique handles this contradiction well. I think. "I did not see them at all, but since the little girls say so, I believe it. But it would have been when I was with the Panis of Sieur de Béréy."

There are more questions. Questions we have heard before.

*Do you know where
Claude Thibault is?
Why did he flee?*

There are more answers. Answers we
have heard before.

* * *

"She makes sense. She contradicts
herself. Who can say what is truth and what
is falsehood?"

I am having a confrontation of my own.
Madeleine and Sidonie are grilling me about
the day's events, admittedly a noteworthy
day in the course of the trial. Angélique has
slipped. Or has she? My wife, as always, is
quick to point out that fear, hunger, pain,
and loneliness can do unheard of things to
mind, body, and soul. Perhaps Angélique is
not caught up so much in a web of lies as in
a life that is unbearable.

Still, this is where we find ourselves.
More than twenty witnesses, more
interrogations and confrontations that I
have ever experienced before, and I am not
sure the road to justice has a clear end in
sight.

"What does that mean for Angélique?"
my wife wants to know.

I remind both these women sitting here
with me in the fading sunlight sipping

lukewarm tea that the French justice system is built on a presumption of guilt. "There is no out here for Angélique unless someone steps forward to confess to starting the fire or we find Claude Thibault."

Sidonie throws her hands in the air. "What is all this with Claude Thibault? This is about Angélique. Why do we waste so much time on this man? This man who is so obviously long gone. He cannot help."

"He can." I say this gently. "If he were to step forward and admit he was behind the fire, the outcome might be different for Angélique."

"How?" This is my wife. There is no confrontation in her tone, rather a genuine interest in understanding what it is I am saying.

"The court presumes arson was not Angélique's idea. If she points a finger of blame at Thibault, or better yet, he presents himself to the authorities, it could well affect her sentence."

"How?" My wife again.

"The court could go easier on her."

Madeleine picks up on my use of the auxiliary verb. "Could."

"Could." I refuse to expand. That is a road that leads to no good for me.

"Not would." And there it is. How one letter makes a world of difference.

There is nothing I can do but acknowledge the point Madeleine is making. "Not would."

Sidonie wants to talk process and timeline. I don't know if this reassures her there is a proper path to justice or if she is looking to see any light whatsoever at the end of this journey. I explain that the court must conclude the trial, then it must render a verdict and a punishment. Both could be appealed to the Conseil Supérieur in Québec City.

"Could, not would." I say this to the blank space in front of my teacup. I do not look at my wife. This will not be an easy night for me.

"Can she go free?"

Sidonie's plea is heartfelt. I am somewhat surprised. I did not think she and Angélique were that close. Perhaps this has more to do with Angélique being nearer to her station in life than all the mistresses in the world.

"We must not get ahead of ourselves. It is one day at a time."

"It has been many days." Sidonie sounds petulant. I understand her frustration. I also understand the need for each step in the judicial process. Justice takes time.

I start to explain the need for patience, but Madeleine waves away my explanation.

"Oui. Oui. Justice. Thoroughness. Procedure. You have mentioned this all before."

She hesitates for a second.

"You know what's missing?"

Sidonie and I look at her. She has our attention. "Madame de Francheville."

"What do you mean? She testified. It did not look good for Angélique."

Madeleine nods. "But she has not confronted her slave, the woman she has accused of burning down most of the merchants' quarter?"

So much for procedure.

* * *

We are walking home arm in arm. If my wife was annoyed with me, all is forgiven now. This would be pleasant if it were not for the smoke that clings to our clothes and the weight that lays heavy on our hearts.

"Everyone is trying to do the right thing."

Madeleine looks at me. "That is all anyone can do."

I squeeze her arm. This conversation could have gone much differently. My wife smiles at me. Something lingers in the corners. "Did you, perhaps, forget anything this week?"

It is a puzzling question, and it is, of course, not a question. I review my week, at work, at home, in the courtyard of the Hôtel-Dieu, with my wife, with bébé. I have forgotten nothing. To be precise, I cannot remember what I have forgotten. Madeleine will tell me.

"Maman, Papa."

Dear Lord, I forgot to write my parents. How could I have forgotten. I am upset with myself. This is unacceptable, no matter how important my job or my family here.

Now it is Madeleine who squeezes my arm. "I sent them a letter. I told them how busy you were. How you miss them. How we tell le bébé all about them."

I love this woman.

* * *

May 31, 1734

Cher Maman, Papa,

I must start with an apology. The trial has me preoccupied. I spend my days buried in paper, or pondering black marks on roof shingles, or sharing my lunch with a man who literally lives in a prison. It is important to understand what happened on April 10 when Montréal went up in flames, but nothing is more important than my family.

I ache to take Madeleine and le bébé back home. To meet you. She would love Acadie. If only she could see the verdant forests, touch the rich, fertile soil, dip her toes in the waters that hug the coastline and feed the bay every day. Perhaps one day. Perhaps soon.

Now you will be preparing the fields for planting. Do you have oxen this year to help break the soil? Have you begun sowing? Will there be barley and wheat this year?

I can see Maman in the garden, giving her tomatoes, carrots, and turnip a head start on the growing season. Perhaps she is milking the cows, although I know that is not her favorite chore. I believe the cows agree.

The ice is breaking up in the river here. Soon canoes will arrive in greater force; the fur trade will be in full swing. There will be goods arriving on a regular basis. I am hoping for some fresh fruit. An orange would be nice, but nothing compares to the apples plucked off the trees in Acadie.

I do not remember if I have mentioned Sidonie. She is a servant girl who worked next door to Madame de Francheville. She has been helping me answer some questions since the fire. She can speak freely with other servants and slaves. We meet in the courtyard of the Hôtel-Dieu. The sisters always have tea. Madeleine brings some food. Sidonie is always hungry. I swear she is eating for two.

Most people on rue Saint-Paul have found alternate accommodations, but this is temporary. The rebuilding is under way, but it will be a slow process. It may be years before the new hospital is open. But we carry on. What else can we do?

Perhaps there are those who say that of Angélique, but I watch her in court. This is not about going through the motions. This is about fighting for your life.

Your loving son,
Philippe

PS Le bébé is now the size of two little pumpkins!

Chapter 24
Confrontation
Wednesday, June 2, 1734

There is one confrontation today. I wonder if it goes according to plan. Angélique and her accuser are in agreement.

The accuser is ten-year-old Marguerite de Couagne. What we know most about her is that she likes playing in the mud. The young girl seems composed, but then what do I know about the composure of young girls. I have lots of nieces, but none have been brought to a gaol to face an accused arsonist.

The highlights of her deposition:

> *She was outside the day of the fire.*
>
> *Claude Thibault did speak to her on several occasions prior to the fire but not anytime on the day of the fire.*
>
> *She did not say that Angélique said her mistress would not sleep in her house that night. It was the Panis slave Marie-Manon who told her that.*

She did not see Angélique with Claude Thibault the day of the fire. She had seen them together prior to this, including the day after Thibault was released from jail.

* * *

"There is nothing new here. Indeed, it is the very same deposition the girl gave when she was deposed several weeks ago."

Rolant nods. He is sitting on the other side of the desk. We are reviewing my notes from this morning. "This is thoroughness. It is to be commended, but it cannot last. The end is in sight."

"We seem to be missing one witness."

Rolant looks at me. Through me. "There has been an issue. That issue will soon be resolved.

So, Madame de Francheville will confront her slave in court.

* * *

I have tidied away the papers and am thinking about the midday meal when I realize Rolant is still here. "Is there more we need to discuss?"

"There may be."

I wait. My superior is a thoughtful man. Whatever else we need to talk about he will tell me in his own time. I know it will be respectful.

"I am surmising. I cannot stress that enough. I am surmising that the court will soon render a verdict. There is only one verdict to render."

I am not sure I agree, but I will defer to the men more learned than me, including the one standing before me. Rolant continues to shape his words with care. "The decision will be appealed."

The appeal judgment would be rendered by the Conseil Supérieur in Québec. It is the foremost judicial body in New France. Their decision will be final.

"I think you should go."

I hear the words from Rolant's mouth. I have no idea what they mean. My confusion is obvious. "To Québec."

"You want me to go to Québec? To the town?" This is not me asking questions as much as it is me confirming I have heard the words he said correctly.

My superior smiles. "It will take you about a week, perhaps longer. You will go by canoe."

"Why?" This is not a challenge. It is me trying to understand what purpose I would serve in Québec.

"Once the appeal court renders its decision, you will return here to inform the tribunal and the notaries about what has been determined. We must be prepared."

Rolant has said all he needs to say. We must, indeed, be prepared. Perhaps for the worst.

* * *

"Why?"

Madeleine asks me the same question I asked of Rolant. I give the same answer. I also reassure her I will be home long before le bébé arrives.

My wife understands the need for me to leave; she may even be proud I have been asked to do this, but we have not been apart before. This will not be easy.

* * *

There is the usual lukewarm tea and heated conversation. Madeleine still struggles with my upcoming absence. Sidonie struggles to understand why the court's decision must be appealed at all.

"It ensures fairness and justice. It gives the evidence every opportunity to be carefully weighed."

"Then why bother with a trial?" Sidonie asks. "Why do we go through this only to go through it all over again?"

"The appeal court will be quick," I note. This seems to appease Sidonie – and Madeleine.

217

I explain the role of the Conseil, officially established in 1663 when King Louis XIV ended the rule of the French West India Company and took over direct control of New France. It advises and assists the Governor of New France in the administration of the colony and oversees judicial matters.

"That is a job I would like," says Madeleine, and we all laugh.

"You would make an excellent member of the Conseil, but sadly, you are not eligible." The council is composed of senior officials and representatives of the Church. The Governor, the Intendant, the Bishop, and other key members of the community sit on the court. There are twelve in all.

"Twelve men will decide what happens to a woman they have never met." Madeleine tries to say this without judgment. She fails.

"They will meet her." Now I have the attention of both women.

"You will travel with Angélique!" Sidonie is aghast.

"No, I will leave before she is escorted to the court. I will have several hours head start, perhaps a day."

"Is it dangerous?" Sidonie asks the question my wife has been reluctant to ask.

"No," I lie. "It is perfectly safe."

Chapter 25
Judgment
Friday, June 4, 1734

Thérèse de Couagne de Francheville does not want her day in court. She has refused to see Angélique ever again. She wants nothing to do with the woman who once lived in her house. With the woman she owns.

One does not, however, say "no" to the court. Judge Raimbault issues an official ordinance compelling Madame de Francheville to appear. He goes so far as to deliver that message in person. Madame de Francheville now stands before us.

Angélique fires the first volley. "I have severe reproaches to make against this witness and shall wish her ill will all of her life." The slave admonishes her owner for accusing her of starting the fire. She also denies going up to the attic on the day of the fire, except in the morning when she went up with her mistress. She likewise denies seeing Thibault on the evening of the fire; it was more than eight days earlier that she last saw him at the house.

I am writing with the speed of a startled horse. I stop abruptly. Angélique is mistaken. Or she is lying.

Madame de Francheville disputes much of what Angélique has to say. She contends Angélique brought food to Thibault in the gaol seven to eight days prior to his release. Learning of this, Madame de Francheville forbade her from giving the man anything.

Madame de Francheville is done. Angélique is not.

* * *

It is nine o'clock, and Angélique is once again in the criminal seat facing little Amable Monière. First though, she is facing the full court. There is, I feel, a shift in the atmosphere. The energy in the room is palpable. The questioning takes turns and paths not previously followed.

"Where did you obtain the eight knives and the pair of scissors found on you when you were arrested?"

"The knives came from Madame de Francheville. The packet came undone in the hospital garden and seeing everyone going to gather them up, I placed them in a box." That box, Angélique continues, was found by Sister Boutier who wanted to take it away, so Angélique put the utensils in her pocket.

When asked why she didn't return the knives, she says she had not yet gone to the house at the time of her arrest. With respect to the scissors, Angélique says they were used earlier in the day to cut out a pair of leg coverings for herself, and she placed them in her pocket.

Suddenly, Judge Raimbault does something he has not done before. He brandishes eight knives and a pair of scissors. "Do you recognize them?"

Angélique does. She points to a black-handled small knife as her own kitchen knife.

I have no idea what is going on. I do not understand why the knives have been introduced, except perhaps to cast Angélique as a thief. It can be added to the litany of aspersions. *Liar. Runaway. Arsonist. Thief.*

Judge Raimbault has moved on. To familiar territory. We are back to Claude Thibault.

"How many times did Thibault enter the house of Madame de Francheville on the eve of the fire? Did he use the knife to smoke?"

Now comes denial, or clarification. Or diversion. "He did not enter either on the day before or two days prior to the fire but only on the day of his release from the gaol."

More movement from the esteemed judge. To unfamiliar territory. Two shovels are thrust before Angélique. "Do you know these?"

She does. The smaller one is for the chamber and the larger one for the kitchen."

"Which of the two shovels did you use to carry embers when the little Amable

Monière saw you with a shovel in your hand filled with embers? You were going upstairs."

I am riveted by the show that is unfolding in the small courtroom. The introduction of physical evidence somehow makes the accusations ring true. Yet, a kitchen knife is just a knife, a shovel only a shovel.

Angélique's anticipated denial reminds me of that reality. "I carried no embers upstairs, either in the morning or the evening."

Now it is not Angélique who is identifying shovels. It is Amable Monière. The little girl says the larger shovel was the shovel she saw. Then she demonstrates how Angélique carried the shovel. There appears to be no duplicity here. Then again, how deceitful can a five-year-old be?

* * *

Deceit seems to be the theme. Judge Raimbault is, once again, inquiring about Claude Thibault's visits to the de Francheville home prior to the fire. Angélique has contended that Thibault last visited the house at least eight days before the fire.

That statement is about to be proven false, as I already knew it to be. With what I will later call a "flourish," Judge Raimbault introduces the register of the gaol. The arrest and release dates are documented: On the fifth day of the month of March the man named Thibault was brought to the royal gaol of this city on the order of Monsieur le Commissaire by four musketeers and a sergeant, and released on the eighth of April under the same order."

Bottom line: Claude Thibault could not have visited eight days prior to the fire. He was in jail. But he could have visited two days before the fire and the day before the fire. As witnesses claimed he did.

It comes down to this. Is Angélique being deliberately deceitful or simply mistaken. Judge Raimbault has made up his mind.

* * *

It is unanimous. Angélique is guilty. Angélique will burn.

The final sentence handed down by the court spells out her punishment in detail. It will be brutal. The question I am still asking: Will it be just?

[E]verything considered, we have declared the said accused, Marie-Joseph Angélique sufficiently guilty and convicted of having set fire to the house of Dame de Francheville

*causing the burning of a
portion of the city. In
reparation for which we
have condemned her to
make honourable amends
disrobed, a noose around
her neck, and carrying in
her hands a flaming torch
weighing two pounds
before the main door and
entrance of the parish
church of this city where
she will be taken and led,
by the executioner of the
high court, in a tumbrel
used for garbage, with an
inscription front and back,
with the word, incendiaire,
and there, bare-headed,
and on her knees, will
declare that she
maliciously set the fire and
caused the said burning,
for which she repents and
asks forgiveness from the
Crown and Court, and this
done, will have her fist
severed on a stake erected
in front of the said church.*

*Following which, she will
be led by the said*

*executioner in the same
tumbrel to the public place
to there be bound to the
stake with iron shackles
and burned alive, her body
then reduced to ashes and
cast to the wind, her
belongings taken and
remanded to the King, the
said accused having
previously been subjected
to torture in the ordinary
and extraordinary ways in
order to have her reveal
her accomplices.*

* * *

Sidonie is inconsolable. Madeleine is disappointed, but pragmatic. I expected the reverse.

We have gathered early in the courtyard of the Hôtel-Dieu. We are not alone. Montréal is abuzz. The streets have clusters of men and women drawn out not so much by the promise of summer but the news of Negress slave. Incendiaire!

"The verdict will stand." I anticipate the question both women are waiting to ask me. My statement is assertive. There is no doubt in my mind the Conseil Supérieur will uphold the verdict. There were twenty-four witnesses called over approximately eight weeks. There is only one way to describe that process: thorough.

The high court will undoubtedly agree. Of that, I am certain. "What they may amend," I say to the two women hanging on my every word, "is the sentence itself."

"She could go free!" I am not sure if Sidonie is excited at the prospect or appalled by it. Perhaps both.

I shake my head. "Marie-Joseph Angélique will die for the crime of arson. That death may be less brutal than the decision rendered here today has decreed."

"It is brutal, isn't it." My wife is speaking to us, and through us.

"Justice comes with a price."

"Does it have to be so inhumane?" There will be no appeasing Madeleine on this issue. "They are going to cut off her hand and throw her in a fire – after they torture her."

"Mais, non!" There is no ambiguity in Sidonie's response this time. There is simply horror.

* * *

We are startled by a thump on our table. It is followed by raucous laughter. Henri Geôlier has somehow tracked me down. The question is less "how" and more "why."

"It's time for us to go. We must grab some food first, then head down to the canoes. We want to get as much light as we can."

I have no idea why Monsieur Geôlier is going on this trek with me. I find, though, I am relieved that he is. Madeleine may be feeling the same way. She rises, takes his arm. "I will pack you a big lunch. There will be enough for later in the day."

* * *

The canoes are bigger than I expected. In hindsight this makes sense. They would need to be large to carry furs and supplies. They are also very light. The white birch bark is resilient in the water without being a burden to carry on land.

We are several hours into our journey. The river is swift, and we are making good time. The weather is mild; the sun gives us a little heat and much more light. Our plan is to travel until dark when we will settle in for the night. Until then, we paddle.

Monsieur Geôlier is an excellent travelling companion. There are four of us in the canoe: two guides and the two of us. The guides are quiet. That may be their nature, or it may be that the jailer dominates the conversation. For which I am grateful. Monsieur Geôlier regales us with tales from his youth, from the prison cells, from his personal escapades. Before I am aware, we are heading for land and preparing for nightfall.

227

In the few hours since we left Montréal, we have found a rhythm. We make camp along the riverbank and quickly erect a simple shelter. One of the guides starts a fire; the other arrives with a net full of fish. We will eat well tonight. The fire keeps us warm and wards off animals who might otherwise make their way to our bedsides.

I pull a blanket over me, and I am asleep.

Chapter 26
Appeal
Saturday, June 12, 1734

I had not expected to enjoy this journey, but I am. There is an ease to being outdoors, to moving with and through the environment. You must be sharp, but you can also relax. Here you breathe deeply. I breathe in the beauty of the land and water that surrounds me. The trees are full, the earth is rich and moist, the water clear and cold. There is an ache in my heart. I think of Acadie.

* * *

It takes us seven nights to reach our destination. We have been provided with papers introducing us. We make our way to the quartier de palais. This is where the intendant lives. It is also where the courthouse and the prison can be found. Here there are also shipyards, storehouses, an armoury, and a chapel.

We are taken to our accommodations: simple rooms with the basic necessities. Food is also provided.

Now we wait.

*　*　*

The wait is not long. Angélique arrives almost in our wake. She is taken to the prison, shackled, where she remains until this morning when she is brought before the Conseil Supérieur. Most of the members of the Conseil have turned out. This is unusual.

"So, they have heard of our slave, eh?" says Monsieur Geôlier. He laughs. Another tale to tell his companions on another trip.

*　*　*

Angélique is interrogated. The Conseil listens. The Conseil deliberates.

We have the canoe loaded and ready to go. As soon as the sentence is announced we will be on our way.

As it turns out, we will have plenty of daylight to travel.

Chapter 27
Appeal
Friday, June 18, 1734

Rolant is waiting for me. Monsieur Geôlier and the guides begin to take supplies and provisions out of the canoe. My superior and I begin the walk to the courthouse.

"They have amended the sentence."

"Changes were expected. Are they significant?"

I do not know the answer to this question. "They are less brutal."

* * *

The Conseil Supérieur calls for Marie-Joseph Angélique to:

*... make honourable
amends disrobed, a rope
around her neck, holding
in her hands a flaming
torch weighing two pounds
before the door and main
entrance of the parish
church of the said city of
Montréal, where she will*

231

*be led by the executor of
the high court and there on
her knees state and declare
in a loud and intelligible
voice that she maliciously
and defiantly and wrongly
set the said fire for which
she is repentant, ask
forgiveness from god, the
king and the court.*

*This done she is to be taken
to the public square of the
said City of Montreal to be
hanged until dead at the
gallows erected for this
purpose and then her dead
body is to be placed on a
flaming pyre and burned
and her ashes cast to the
wind, her belongings taken
and confiscated by the
King.*

*Prior to this the said
Marie-Joseph Angélique is
to be subjected to torture in
the ordinary and
extraordinary ways in
order to have her reveal
her accomplices.*

* * *

The courts have spoken. Two courts. Two towns. Two reviews of the evidence. Their conclusions may vary in the details but not in the ultimate rendering. Marie-Joseph Angélique is guilty of arson, a crime punishable by death. And she will die.

The tea is untouched. The conversation non-existent. Sidonie and Madeleine are ensconced in their own thoughts, as am I. We sit like statues, unmoving yet fundamentally moved. I am not sure why this trial has affected us the way it has. Perhaps it is the proximity to the offence. To the offender. Perhaps it is, somewhere beneath the skin, a prickle. *Is she guilty?*

The courts say she is. I trust the courts. I trust the people who work in this system, and I trust the process. Yet no person, no process is infallible. Have we been fallible?

Sidonie is the first to speak and when she speaks, she unknowingly answers my question with a resounding "No." Frankly, I appreciate the reassurance especially from the young servant girl. There were times I felt she was convinced of Angélique's innocence.

"This is done. At last. Angélique will get what she deserves as harsh as that punishment my be."

"You believe she is guilty?" Madeleine asks.

"I believe she deserves to die. If not for the fire, then for everything else."

Sidonie sees our shock. That we would consider killing someone for a crime they did not commit is unconscionable. "You do not live in my world. Survival is paramount. That is what Angélique tried to do. She failed. Now she pays the price."

Madeleine plays the diplomat. "In your heart, do you imagine she is guilty of this crime?"

Sidonie looks at us both. She sips her cold tea. She rises from her chair. "In my world, there is no time to imagine what might be."

* * *

In her inimitable way, Madeleine is moving on. She has accepted what at one time was unacceptable. She is now wondering if I can do the same. "In your heart, do you imagine she is guilty of this crime?"

"In my heart, I do not want her to be."

234

Chapter 28
Brodequins
Saturday, June 19, 1734

I am clearing away the remnants of my role as special rapporteur. I am putting my notes, findings, observations in order should they ever be required. I have the three shingles on my desk. Still a mystery. Or not. Who is to say what happens in a fire, when lives and possessions go up in flames.

"You have done a good job. Do not forget that."

Rolant has somehow come up behind me. "The court is satisfied it has reached a fair and just verdict. I am satisfied we left no," he pauses with a slight smile, "shingle unturned."

I smile back. It is time to move on.

* * *

"I will miss this." Monsieur Geôlier is being sentimental between mouthfuls of cold stew.

I realize I agree with him. "Something tells me we have not had our last lunch. I will ask Madeleine to pack a little extra at least once a week."

The laugh, the thumping are back. "Bon."

"How is she doing?" It is an inane question, but my lunch colleague understands what I am really asking.

"Some people condemned to die spend their days howling, others crying, others shaking. It is all acceptance. She has accepted this."

"What do you think it means that she has not implicated Claude Thibault? Do people in jail condemned to death usually do that?"

"Some do. Some do not. It makes no difference. He is gone. We will not find him."

"I thought you believed a woman was hiding him."

"Women like men like him. They do foolish things when they like men. And he likes women. Your young servant girl is his type."

"Because she is pretty?"

"Because she is breathing." The laugh is back. My desk resounds with the thumping of his hand.

* * *

Monsieur Geôlier is lingering. He takes time to wipe his mouth with the back of his hand, then wipe his hands on his pants.

"It is good you care. Sometimes that may make you see what you want to see."

236

I have heard this before. The evidence against Angélique is circumstantial, but there is much of it. Then there is little Amable. Why would a five-year-old lie about a slave carrying embers to the attic? I must face reality.

The jailer is trying to be kind. I appreciate the kindness. "You are right. I must not worry how Angélique is doing. I will not ask you anymore."

Henri Geôlier stops wiping and laughing and thumping. He looks at me. "You are not asking the right questions."

* * *

Monday.
So, it has been decided. Angélique will die in two days. Rolant has arrived to review the process with me. There is little to review: torture, church, hanging, burning. I will have no direct role, but there is an expectation that all members of the court will watch the procession through the town, will witness the hanging and the subsequent burning of the arsonist. It is a show of faith in the system and a show of support for those who have to make life-and-death decisions.

* * *

I do not keep this information from Madeleine. There is no need. It will be public knowledge soon enough if it isn't already.

237

The streets will be crowded. There will be no avoiding the subject or the spectacle.

My wife pours another cup of tea. From somewhere some fruit to savour. "I am fine," I assure my wife. We have not gone into the lower town. We have not gone to see Sidonie, if she is even there. Somehow it feels as if our journey together has come to an end. There is nothing more I need from her. There is nothing more I can give her.

"It was helpful for both of you."

Madeleine is right. This was not a friendship, was never going to be a friendship, but it was friendly. "We must move on."

Apparently le bébé agrees. There is a big kick. Madeleine's belly bounces. We laugh. It feels good to laugh. My wife takes my hand. "We must move on."

I am not sure why she is repeating herself, but I nod. Now both my hands are in hers. "You are not hearing me. We must move on."

Chapter 29
Brodequins
Monday, June 21, 1734

My desk is empty. There are no papers, no quills, no ink. There are no shingles, no records, no court documents. Yet here I sit in my chair behind my desk feeling somehow as if I have failed as special rapporteur. As if I have somehow failed my superior. As if somehow, I have failed Angélique.

It is still early in the morning. The sun has risen. So has the hangman. Before he makes his way to the lower town, however, and the hanging post, Mathieu Léveillé must first get a confession from Angélique and an admission she had an accomplice. The court is not giving up on Claude Thibault. I have.

It will not take long to get what the court wants. The brodequins are very effective. Misleadingly and accurately called laced boots or tight boots, this particular form of torture involves packing a person's legs between narrow boards tightly bound. Wooden wedges are then pounded between board and human flesh. Bone breaks. Boards do not.

I am close enough to the interrogation chamber to hear the screams. I feel it is my responsibility to see this through. I sit silently behind my desk. Finally, the screams stop.

* * *

"You must eat. And drink." Monsieur Geôlier is standing before me. He places bread and cheese on the desk. He hands me a flask.

"It is a little early to imbibe."

"Not today."

The jailer is right. Today is a day of exceptions. Or not. Perhaps this is a day like any other in its predictability.

I drink. The liquid is sweet. It warms my throat. I feel my legs again.

"She has confessed to starting the fire."

"There was never any doubt."

"That she started the fire or that she would confess."

"The brodequins are very effective." I sidestep the question. Perhaps because I do not know the answer. Perhaps because it does not matter.

"You wanted it to be someone else."

Monsieur Geôlier, once again, is right. I smile. It is the smile of one friend to another. "I thought perhaps the fire started next door."

"Aah, the Panis slave."

"Yes. Marie-Manon. But she could not have done it. Sidonie saw her in the street before the fire alert was sounded."

240

"Why did you think she would start the fire?"

"I thought it might be an accident."

My friend nods. "There should never have been wooden shingles on that roof. Perhaps that is the real crime."

* * *

"Do you want to know what happened?"

Monsieur Geôlier waits while I ponder his question. Part of me wants to know what Angélique said inside the walls of the interrogation room. Part of me does not. This is a human life. I would like to leave her with some dignity. Finally, I tell myself, as special rapporteur, I must follow this investigation through to the end.

"She did not give up Claude Thibault."

"Oh, la vache!"

The jailer wants to laugh at my profanity, to thump my desk. He refrains.

"She said she was innocent. They inserted a wedge. She said she wanted to die. She said she did this and no one else."

"Do you think she was telling the truth?"

"I was not in the room. I do not know if she was being honest. I do know she was in pain. She withstood two more wedges. With the fourth wedge, she asked to be hanged. She said, 'It is me alone.'"

Thus ended la question ordinaire. Four strikes. This did not, I know, end the torture.

Four more strikes. La question extraordinaire.

Monsieur Geôlier's voice comes as if from a distance. "With the first strike, she said, 'Put me to death.' With the second strike, she said, 'It's me alone.' With the third, 'Hang me, it's me.' With the last, 'It's me, with a grilling pan. No one advised me to do it; it was a thought, an evil thought that came to me.'"

We are surrounded by silence. The jailer does not break it. I find myself thinking not about Angélique but about the jailer. The layers that define him. Layers I failed to see. I wonder what else I failed to see.

"Was it over then?"

"The brodequins were done. As the law requires. The interrogation continued."

"Did she accuse Thibault?"

"She did not. Her last words: 'It is I, sirs. Put me to death. I have no accomplice.'"

* * *

Angélique is heading to her death. There is nothing anyone can do now but wait.

The waiting proves difficult for me. I cannot imagine what it must be like for Angélique. I do not want to imagine this.

I make my way to the lower town. The execution is hours away and, for now, the streets are quiet. I find myself where I have found myself so often these last weeks, in the garden of the Hôtel-Dieu. It is empty except for one sister who is tidying the yard, perhaps in preparation for the many who will arrive as the day opens into evening.

"We have not seen you here lately."

"I have been away to Québec. I am just back these past few days."

The sister smiles at me. I am ashamed to admit I do not know her name despite the many times I have seen her here, smiled at her, wished her a good day. "Our garden gets fewer visitors these past few days. It is, I pray, a sign we are moving on. Like your friend."

The sister sees the surprise on my face. "You do not know. Your friend, the servant girl, she has left her post."

"Is everything all right?"

A hand pats my arm. "I did not mean to startle you. Sidonie seemed happy when she told me. She is moving away. A fresh start with her family. This is what we all need, non."

* * *

I do not want to be here although I understand why I must. Madeleine wants to be here although she understands why she cannot. Le bébé has decided this for her. She is having pain, but not birthing pain. This is just the little one speaking out. He does not want his Maman to witness this. I agree with him. (And return to my original prediction that the pumpkin is a boy.)

This is spectacle. Angélique is being wheeled through the streets of Montréal in a cart. In her hand, she holds a burning torch, an acknowledgement of her crime. Someone, as is tradition, has stripped her bare and placed a white chemise over her body.

This is humiliation. The hand cart that carries Angélique on her final journey is usually used to transport garbage. I look at the people who look at Angélique as she makes her way to the hanging post, and I wonder if this is what they see: garbage. If this somehow gives them a sense of justice. On Angélique's white shirt is embroidered: incendiaire. A life has been reduced to a single word.

This is revenge. We have won. Justice has prevailed. Angélique stops at Notre-Dame, one last chance to make things right with God, the King, and the crowds who throng the streets. Her amende honorable. I do not know if Angélique believes in God, our god. I can hear my mother's voice, "There is only one god." Would the Negress slave agree?

This is power. We have decided Angélique is guilty. She most likely is. The evidence, such as it is, supports this conclusion. There are no other suspects. Does that give us the right to decide what happens to her soul?

On Monday, June 21, 1734, Marie-Joseph Angélique is hanged in front of the house she is said to have burned. Her body will be displayed on a gibbet for two hours. Then it will be placed on a pyre. Her ashes will be collected and scattered to the wind. It will be the final degradation.

* * *

The streets are crowded. Few people have left. They are waiting for the final spectacle, the final humiliation, the finale revenge.

I straighten my shoulders, breathe in. This is what must be done, but it does not have to sit well on the soul or the heart. Mine ache.

There is a crowd of people in every direction. I find it difficult to move, to breathe. The fire is lit. There is a moment when the flames take me back to that night in April when the merchants' quarter burned. Now it is Angélique going up in flames. I wish her peace on this her final journey.

My wishes have fallen on deaf ears. Angélique's ashes are scattered to the wind. Surely this goes beyond justice. This is sacrilege. This is to deny someone entry into heaven. To make it impossible for body and soul to enter intact means body and soul cannot enter at all.

My duty is done. I turn to head home. A profile across the street catches my attention. I am not sure why, but any distraction is welcome. The distraction is

245

Sidonie. She sees me. I nod. I think I should make my way to her, but the street is crowded, and our time is done.

Sidonie turns back. A man is standing beside her. She reaches down and when she straightens, she is holding a child. She turns back to look at me. She smiles.

A shiver runs down my spine.

* * *

Madeleine does not ask me about the day. She wants to know, but she wants to respect this time to let me understand what it is I am feeling. For the most part, it is confusion.

Over dinner, I tell my wife what the sister has told me about Sidonie and about seeing Sidonie. I am grappling with something. I do not know what. Madeleine tries to help me draw out my thoughts.

"You think the infant is Sidonie's."

"I do."

"Is that so surprising?"

It is a good question. Why would Sidonie not have a child? She is young, she is pretty, she is nice. The question is really why did I not know Sidonie had a child?

"We did not really talk about our lives. We talked about Angélique." My wife is being diplomatic.

"Perhaps we were remiss."

"Perhaps. But it is why we were there. It is why Sidonie was there."

246

I think back to the first time I met Sidonie. Before the fire. A few moments on a stoop as I entered the de Béréy house, a few moments as I left. My impression of a young woman. Quiet. Deferential. Plump.

"She was pregnant."

My wife stops pouring the tea. "You have jumped ahead."

"I'm thinking back to when I first met Sidonie. She was full and round."

"She was pregnant."

"I remember when we first met her in the garden after the fire that she looked thinner, tired."

"She had the baby."

We may be right. Perhaps she was pregnant. Perhaps she gave birth after the fire. Perhaps she did not wish us to know. But what of it?

"You think there is something more."

"I think there is more I must think about."

* * *

June 21, 1734

Cher Maman, Papa,

I write, as always, to send my love and to tell you we are all fine. Madeleine is full with le bébé. We cannot wait for her to arrive. (I have changed my mind. I am now convinced the little one is a little girl.)

I am also writing to get my thoughts in order. There are things I need to think about more carefully, and my letters home offer a time for reflection and consideration. I hope you do not think I am taking advantage of you or your love.

Angélique died today. I knew that was coming. I also knew there was no way to prepare. I was not prepared. My first execution. I hope it is my last. The slave was hanged, burned. Her ashes scattered. There will be no eternal peace.

Some will call this justice. Some will call it retribution. It may be both. It may be that both are acceptable. Yet this does not sit right with me. I miss the farm, having my hands in the earth. Things had more well-defined shapes; there were fewer shadows.

It is the shadows where I seem to spend most of my time lately. I am struggling to make sense of what I know about Sidonie. I told you about her. The servant girl who has been helping me understand what happened the night of the fire.

She has left her post. Moving away I have been told. I saw her briefly in the crowd today with un bébé. It appears to be her bébé. As Madeleine points out, she is mature enough to have a child and under no obligation to share this information with us. Yet we did share part of our day for many days. Did I not care enough to ask about her life? Was this strictly quid pro quo? As we sipped tea and enjoyed some fruit, did we not connect as people as well as sources of information?

Is this what is troubling me? Or are there implications beyond the surprise I feel? When I was hunting for Claude Thibault one of men said he had gotten a servant girl pregnant. Was that servant girl Sidonie? If it was, it changes everything.

It means our shared trust was an illusion. A shadow. It means the baby was simply not a topic that never came up but a deliberate omission. But so, what if she had a child with Thibault? Clearly he slept with other women, and I dare say, stirred deep feelings. Despite her torture, Angélique never gave him up.

If Sidonie felt the same way, would she likewise go to extremes to protect him? Would she have secreted him away, somewhere her family had a cottage or a piece of land?

Mon Dieu. She knew where he was even as she looked me in the eye and said he was surely long gone from Montréal. I believed her conviction. Indeed, it never occurred to me that she would have reason to lie.

If she lied about this, what else did she lie about? Quite simply, the answer is everything. I am being unfair perhaps, but I must follow this path. I know I am following it too late.

Where does it ultimately lead? To Sidonie lying about Angélique. That may be, but those lies are surely irrelevant. Sidonie did not have a direct conversation with Angélique the day of the fire. She was not called as a witness. There were twenty-four witnesses. There was admittedly, innuendo, but it was consistent inference. And there was little Amable.

So why the subterfuge? Was she hiding only Claude Thibault? Or something more?

That is the question I must answer. That answer will not come this evening. The moon is already out and settled in for the night. I must follow. It is time for me to say adieu.

Your loving son,
Philippe

PS Thank you for listening. I will kiss le bébé for you both.

Chapter 30
Incendiaire
Tuesday, June 22, 1734

The prison is dank, dark. Prisons are, by their very purpose, not places of rest and repose, but this is chillier, eerier than I remember. I realize I have not been in this part of the gaol for some time. I have spent much more time in the small, attached chamber but have had little need in recent weeks to venture further past those walls.

I hear Monsieur Geôlier before I see him. He is yelling at one of the prisoners. The tone is matter of fact; there is no animosity. There is no flexing of muscles to reaffirm who has the power here. I smile. That is in keeping with the Henri Geôlier I know. He is a man comfortable in his own skin.

My presence disconcerts him. Only for a second. Then there is the familiar laugh and the thump. This time his huge hand lands on my back.

"I have plenty of lunch and thought you'd like to join me."

The jailer plays along as I knew he would. There is a free meal in this game of mine, whatever that might be. There is also human curiosity and, I like to think, a willingness to support a friend.

Lunch is a disparate meal. I eat in silence and Monsieur Geôlier tells tales of his latest prisoners between mouthfuls of ham, bread, and fruit. With the last bite gone, he looks at me. "Now we shall get to business."

"There is no business," I say, and hesitate. The laughter and the thumping are back. The table bears the brunt of his hand this time. I cannot help but smile, at him, at me, at this thing that has become a friendship based on mutual respect. Who would have guessed?

"I saw Sidonie yesterday. With a child."

If the jailer is surprised, he does not show it. "That is to be expected, eh. She is ripe."

"Yet she never mentioned a child to me. I think she was pregnant when I first met her, just before the fire."

"You think she hid it from you."

"If she did, it raises other questions."

"Questions you did not ask."

* * *

I realize what I have come to respect about Monsieur Geôlier: he does not judge others. We are who we are. If I missed a question, or several, it is what it is. Let us get to the matter at hand rather than waste time on recriminations.

"The child concerns you."

"I think it is Claude Thibault's."

"Merde."

We spend the next ten minutes debating the possible parentage of Sidonie's child, if it even is her child. In the end, we decide to follow this line of thinking and see where it takes us. I do not know where that is, but it makes me uneasy.

"If she lied about this, what else did she lie about?"

"If she lied." The jailer has a point. One I dismiss.

"We are splitting hairs."

"It is an important hair."

"She did not lie about Angélique," Monsieur Geôlier points out. "Her reports are either irrelevant or there were other, better witnesses."

"She may have lied about Claude Thibault. She may have helped him hide."

The jailer nods, and shrugs. "So what. He is gone now. Perhaps he escaped death. Perhaps his life will be hell on earth. We can do nothing about this."

I understand what he is doing: trying to make me feel better about myself, less responsible perhaps for having missed clues in front of my face. "I trusted her."

"That was a mistake."

Now it is my turn to laugh, at the simplicity and accuracy of the statement, at myself. My laughter is met with two raised eyebrows. "The question I should be asking is, 'Does any of this matter?'"

"Only if you think she started the fire or knows who does."

"I was convinced it was Marie-Manon. That it was an accident."

"What unconvinced you?"

"Sidonie saw her from inside the house. She was on the street with Angélique and others."

"So Sidonie says."

"Why would she lie about that?"

And there it is. The thing that has been bothering me. The thread I have been reluctant to pull, laid bare.

* * *

Madeleine has prepared a lovely meal. I barely remember eating. She engages in conversation. I barely remember what we talk about. As my tea gets cold on the table in front of me, my wife says she is going for a walk. Alone. I do not blame her.

When she returns, she is not alone. Monsieur Geôlier is with her. Without a word, my wife dishes up a plate of stew, hot from the hearth (and much larger than the plate I had). The jailer takes a chair and thumps my back for good measure as he sits.

"I hear you are stewing." He cannot help himself. Laughter bubbles up, boils over, and suddenly there are three of us chuckling with merriment. "That is what we needed, eh."

My wife and I agree. There is wine, compliments of Monsieur Geôlier I'm told. He brushes aside my thanks. "Down to business. You will fret until this is done."

Now it is my wife's hand on my back. The touch is gentle, supportive. "He told me everything."

Everything, of course, is relative. We start at the beginning, and we work our way around to the thread. We pull. We do not worry about proof or belief at this point, we simply tug until the thread unravels.

Sidonie was pregnant.

Sidonie had a child with Claude Thibault.

Sidonie helped the fugitive hide.

We take time to explore the "why" of this last statement. "She will want to marry him," says Monsieur Geôlier. "They always do." He takes one look at my wife and has the decency to blush.

"Perhaps she is looking for stability for her family, an income, support, comfort."

Monsieur Geôlier is willing to buy this argument. So is Madeleine. She has another theory, however. "Sidonie is in love."

It's so simple really. You ache for another human being and that ache drives you to do things and say things you might not otherwise say and do. I smile at my wife, chastened. Monsieur Geôlier is not such a romantic.

"Perhaps. Perhaps not. Either way she is with child and that brings a whole new level

of responsibility and fear. She will not want
to be alone. She will not want the father of
her child in jail."

"But why would her family help?" I ask.
"Why would they jeopardize their safety?
Break the law?"

"Bah," says Monsieur Geôlier. "Our laws
are not their laws. Our laws are for those who
have food on the table every night and a
warm bed. When you cannot guarantee that,
you take risks others would not take."

"There is also shame," says Madeleine.
She is right. The church, the government, the
neighbours next door. All will point a finger
of blame at the woman with child but
without husband.

"The man gets off without reprobation."

Monsieur Geôlier nods his agreement. It
is unclear whether he is agreeing with my
wife or that men should bear no
responsibility for children born outside
marriage. He looks at my wife. And blushes.

There is more wine and more discussion.
It comes down to "So what?" Sidonie lied
about being pregnant, perhaps about
knowing where Claude Thibault was.

"This bothers you still."

The jailer is right. "We have more to
unravel."

"The fire." Madeleine looks at me. "You
think she started the fire."

"Surely not!" says Monsieur Geôlier.

Now it is my wife's turn to smile a
knowing smile. "Sieur, you do not know the

extent to which a woman will go to protect her child."

"How?" asks the jailer.

I rerun our evening conversations in my mind. "She was in the house on the main floor. She heard the call of 'Fire!' She looks out the window. She sees Marie-Manon. She sees Angélique."

"So how do you start a fire from the main floor of a house?" asks the jailer.

"You don't," I say. "You start the fire in the attic. You look out the window of the attic. You see who is in the street. You wait for someone to see the blaze. You run downstairs and into the street."

Incendiaire.

* * *

There is more wine and more discussion. We are agreed and on opposite sides. The key question seems to be not whether Sidonie could have started the fire – accidentally or deliberately – but whether she would let Angélique die for her actions. I do not think she would. (Madeleine and Monsieur Geôlier say I do not want to think she would.) Madeleine thinks without a doubt that the servant would let the slave hang. *She has a child now.*

Monsieur Geôlier has the most extreme view of all. "She did this so Angélique would hang. The competition is out of the way.

Everyone feels justice has been served. All the loose ends have been tied up nicely."

"Except for Thibault," Madeleine points out.

The jailer shrugs this observation off. I am reminded of water on a duck's back. "He is old news now. The slave has hung. Her lover has escaped. Now we rebuild the lower town."

"Do you think we should all move on?" I feel Monsieur Geôlier's eyes on me. I hear Madeleine gasp. I am surrounded by perceptive people.

"Don't be a fool," says the jailer.

"Do what you feel is right," says my wife.

"Don't open this door. All hell will rain down," says the jailer.

"You have to live with yourself," says my wife.

I remain silent.

Chapter 31
Incendiaire
Wednesday, June 23, 1734

I break my silence at roughly 7:30 in the morning. Rolant is at his desk. He can see by the expression on my face, I have something of import to discuss. He closes his door. From a drawer he removes a small bottle of brandy. "I suspect we will need this."

As always, Rolant listens carefully. He asks few questions and offers up no interjections even though I know some of what I say must be disconcerting. When I am finished, Rolant pours us each another brandy and leans back.

"To summarize, Sidonie may have been pregnant. She may have had a child around the time of the fire. That child may be fathered by Claude Thibault. In an effort, perhaps, to protect her family or out of vengeance, she may have started the fire that destroyed our lower town. She may have let Angélique take the blame. Indeed, she may have counted on this. Finally, she may have sheltered the fugitive Thibault until it was safe for one or both of them to leave Montréal."

I nod. Rolant sips. "You have been diligent. You have taken the role of special rapporteur with the seriousness it deserved. Now, it is time for us to be realistic. To be pragmatic. What was the most common word I used just now in my summary?"

The word is *may*.

"You're saying this is all conjecture."

"It is conjecture. That is not to say it is not accurate, but it cannot be proven."

"Do you think we proved Angélique was guilty?" There is no edge to my voice, but the question itself is an edge. I regret it almost instantly. I respect Rolant.

My superior takes no offence, at least none that I can see. "There were twenty-four witnesses who came before the court to testify on some aspect of Angélique's behaviour. There was admitted and dubious behaviour on the part of the accused herself – she did flee, for example. She contradicted herself under interrogation. She confessed."

"And she is dead."

"After great deliberation and a long, thorough process."

"I should let this go."

"There is nothing to let go. Hold on to the fact you went above and beyond. Savour that dedication. Let it be a source of pride."

It is not pride I am feeling. Perhaps one day. Not now. I thank Rolant and start to make my way out of his office. As I reach for the door, my superior coughs softly. "When were you last to the courtyard of the Hôtel-Dieu."

"It has been a few days."

"Perhaps a return trip would bring you some closure."

Chapter 32
Incendiaire
Saturday, June 26, 1734

I make ten more trips to the Hôtel-Dieu. I speak with the sister, of the weather, the restoration, the sad life of Marie-Joseph Angélique. I sip tea in the quiet of the afternoon and the gloaming. I eat lunch there. Once Monsieur Geôlier comes with me. Twice Madeleine and I make our way to the lower town.

There are merchants and builders and servants and children and fur traders and men of the cloth. There is no Sidonie. Until the tenth trip.

It is twilight. I am on my way home from the court. Taking a detour for what I always tell myself will be the last time. Today, it will be.

Sidonie is sitting at the table where we usually sit. Three cups of tea are before her. "I wasn't sure if Madeleine would be joining us."

"She is at home."

"It is about time is it not for le bébé?"

"Very soon now."

"You must be happy. Madeleine must be scared."

"Were you?"

My abrupt shift is amusing to Sidonie. She looks at me and smiles. It does not warm my heart. This is not the demure woman I once thought I knew. There is a hardness here, an assurance I had not seen or that she did not wish me to see. "My birth was easy. Bébé is healthy. I was back at work the next day."

This is not pride or gloating. It is matter of fact. If there ever was a power imbalance between us, it is gone. I do not have the upper hand.

"I understand you have been looking for me. You are concerned perhaps for my well-being?" The smile is back on her lips. The chill in my breast.

"I have been stupid."

"You saw what you wanted to see. You heard what you wanted to hear."

"What should I have seen? Heard?"

"This is a game neither of us has time for. What do you want to know?"

There it is. The invitation and the dismissal. "Did you start the fire?"

"Yes."

"On purpose?"

"Yes."

"Why?

"I have a child Monsieur Archambeau. That child needs a father. Not a father with a lover. Not a father in gaol."

"You wanted Angélique to hang for this."

"It was my hope she would be sold to the West Indies. Gone from our life. That hope did not materialize." Sidonie shrugs her shoulders slightly. "So be it."

"How did you start the fire?"

"Embers in the attic." So, the court was right about the cause of the fire. Wrong about its origin.

"Do you know where Claude Thibault is?"

"I do. He is out of reach."

"Are you not afraid I will tell the police?"

"No." Sidonie takes a long sip of tea. "Tell them. They will do nothing. Because you will also tell them Angélique did not start the fire. You will tell them the court got it wrong. The merchants will be outraged. The court will be disgraced. You will be removed from your position. You will be disbelieved."

Sidonie is right. And wrong. I would like to think I would put doing the right above my personal discomfort. But as the servant, the once-servant, says, I have le bébé on the way.

"What is the point?" Sidonie can see my internal struggle. "There is peace in the town. Things are getting back to normal. You can hear laughter once more. Let it be."

"Why are you telling me all this?"

"Why not? You cannot hurt me now. By tomorrow morning I will be long gone." Sidonie puts down the teacup she has been holding. It makes a soft, sharp crackle. "I want you to stop coming here. I want people in Montréal to forget me. Yet you keep turning up. That is more troublesome than telling you what you want to know."

"What will you do now?"

"Live my life." Sidonie, the one I thought I knew and the one I spoke to for the first time today, looks me in the eye. "I suggest you do the same."

Epilogue

June 28, 1734
Cher Maman, Papa,

I write to send you love – and news. It has been a hard spring in Montréal. My first spring, and my last. By the time you receive this letter, Madeleine and I will be on our way east to Acadie. To home.

This is a decision that has been a while in the making and was made in an instant. It is the right decision. Montréal is not my home. It never will be. I could possibly be content here with Madeleine and our family, and work that satisfies. But that work satisfies less now. It is time to come home.

Le bébé has grown to the size of three small pumpkins – I do not jest. But we are hopeful she will stay warm in Madeleine's belly until we arrive. We have settled on names. If it is a girl, we will call her Henriette. If it is a boy, Henri.

We will name the little one after Monsieur Geôlier. My friend. Of all I have come to like and admire about Montréal, I will miss the jailer the most. Madeleine invited him to dinner to say good-bye and to tell him his memory will live on in our child. He laughed and he thumped the table. When he thought we were not looking, he wiped away a tear.

The house has been packed up. Everything safely stored and ensconced in trunks. We are ready to travel.

I have done much the same, internally, with the trial of Marie-Joseph Angélique. It has taught me much about the thoroughness and conviction of the court. It has also taught me about preconception and singular sight. I am looking forward to working in the earth. To putting my hands in soil and reaping the just rewards of that labour.

I am also aware of other tensions here in this part of New France. The British are always a breath away, and we are on tenterhooks. It is not this way in Acadie. There we have found détente. We work almost side by side. There is a mutual acceptance of our differences, but they do not sever us.

It is time to come home. To Acadie. We will be safe there. Your loving son,

Philippe

The End

donalee Moulton is an award-winning freelance journalist. She has written articles for print and online publications across North America, including *Chatelaine, Lawyer's Daily, The National Post,* and *Canadian Business.*

Her first mystery book *Hung out to Die* was published in 2023. *Conflagration* is her second mystery novel. donalee's short story "Swan Song" was one of 21 selected for publication in *Cold Canadian Crime.* It was reprinted in Black Cat Weekly and Mystery Most International Anthology. Her literary short story "Moist" was published in *After Dinner Conversation* and *The Antigonish Review.* donalee is also the author of *The Thong Principle: Saying What You Mean and Meaning What You Say* and co-authored *Celebrity Court Cases: Trials of the Rich and Famous.*

donalee lives in Halifax happily surrounded by family, friends, pets, and words of all shapes, sizes, and syllables.